A GIRL'S GUIDE TO LOVE & MAGIC

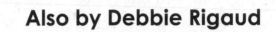

Also by Debbie Rigaud

Truly Madly Royally

Simone Breaks All the Rules

Hope series (with Alyssa Milano)

A GIRL'S GUIDE TO LOVE & MAGIC

DEBBIE RIGAUD

SCHOLASTIC PRESS
NEW YORK

Library of Congress Cataloging-in-Publication Data available

ISBN 978-1-338-68174-1

10 9 8 7 6 5 4 3 2 1   22 23 24 25 26

Printed in the U.S.A.   37

First edition, August 2022

Book design by Yaffa Jaskoll and Maeve Norton

In heartfelt memory of my dynamic,
exuberant dad, Woolly Rigaud.

PROLOGUE

Six Years Ago

What's magical to most is familiar to me.

So when I found myself plunged into dark nothingness except for brilliant points of light all around, I wasn't weirded out. The cosmos was zipping by on either side of me. The only thing I couldn't figure out was if I was standing still or racing through the stars.

I sensed an energy buzzing at my core. It seemed like this place—which felt dreamlike, though it wasn't exactly a dream—had summoned me. I was at home.

Until I wasn't.

I woke to soft tapping sounds. My eyes fluttered open but I lay still, taking a moment to make sense of it all. To catch up.

Where was I? Who was I?

The pulsating sensation of cosmic travel drained from me just as real-world information seeped in: I was Cicely Destin, age nine.

I was in my bedroom. In Flatbush, Brooklyn.

Earth.

The tapping sounds—which I could now clearly make out as rhythmic clapping—drew me out of bed to investigate. Each step across my small room was amplified by the creak of the floorboards and the swish of my Scooby-Doo-print pajamas. I winced at the racket I was making, wondering if my aunt, Tati Mimose, was still here babysitting me. My parents and Grandma Rose had gone on their annual Feast of Saint Anne pilgrimage to honor the Catholic saint at some faraway cathedral.

I was supposed to be asleep and didn't want to be caught out of bed, but my curiosity cared nothing for consequences.

I reached my door, cracked it open, and peeked down the hall to the living room. That's when I observed something I never had seen before—a magic that was truly *magical* to me.

Tati Mimose stood above a dancing fire that burned in a metal basin, one sinewy arm raised and her beautiful face glowering. The licking blue flames had nothing on the fire behind my aunt's eyes. She hadn't even looked this intense when she dominated the *Soul Train* line at our last neighborhood block party.

My aunt was mesmerizing on a regular day, when she'd hold court in our spice-scented kitchen, laughing and trash-talking to a rapt audience of my mom and Grandma Rose, while I giddily wobbled around in her high-heeled shoes. But Tati Mimose in dramatic flame lighting? I could not shut my door on this pageantry any easier than I could stuff streamers back into a confetti popper. How could a person not want to see more, much less a nine-year-old, thick in her mystery-and-fantasy-fandom phase, who imagined herself to be part firecracker Mimose?

The other half of me was all Mom—rigid and disciplined.

Still, I heeded the internal call nudging me forth, farther down the hall to the living room. I stopped, hidden from view. Two other women stood beside my aunt, steadily clap-clapping, all three of them wearing ceremonial white dresses. The coffee table had been cleared to make room for a wooden stool that held the basin.

It was like a stage set for theater, and Tati Mimose was playing the lead role. Her nimble fingers moved with flair as she tied a red satin scarf around her head and spoke in that familiar, rumbling voice she used every time she told me not to forget that I came from a line of powerful women.

"We invoke the power of the ancestors; we call upon my family lwa Ogun the Warrior to bar all evildoers from our presence."

My aunt's shoulders were squared up, her fists balled and her face stern. Were hers not the eyes of someone I loved so dearly, I would be fearful of the intensity flashing from them.

It looks like my aunt, but . . . it doesn't.

Tati Mimose began to dance like she was sparring with a shadow partner. She struck warrior poses while the clappers' chants rang out in Haitian Creole, the catchy melody sung flatly like a playground song. And then my aunt stopped abruptly, swiped her hand in the fiery basin, and grabbed a handful of flames.

I smacked my palm over my mouth in shock.

Wouldn't she burn?

I couldn't say for sure. Everything about the ceremony was new to me. Yes, the tune the women were chanting was similar to the folkloric music my dad listened to when my mom wasn't home. And there, on the mantelpiece—weren't those the prayer candles Grandma Rose kept lit on whatever feast day for whatever patron saint she told all her secrets to?

But Tati Mimose actually touching fire, and dancing like a warrior? I'd never seen that.

This right here was Vodou.

I was pretty sure of that. My family was Haitian. A chipmunk-cheeked boy at school had once said that Haitians and Vodou went hand in hand. He later tried to say he was joking, but that was just because he got caught by the teacher.

You can tell what you're expected to feel about Vodou by the way folks handle the word.

Vo-dou.

Vu-du?

VOODOO!

Sometimes, the word was carted around like a personal item other people played keep-away with. They'd give you taunting glimpses of it, pretend to hand it back, and then yank it away to make a spectacle of you. Eventually, to avoid the humiliation, you'd stop trying to snatch it. You'd even avoid eyeing it, lest anyone remembered it originally belonged to you.

But not if you were Mimose. She'd post a busted selfie on her socials before she'd let anyone shame her about Vodou.

"What's there to hide about an age-old spiritual belief system that's about guiding and protecting its practitioners?" I heard her say to my mom once.

For my mom and everyone else in my family, the word *Vodou* was handled like a ticking bomb—carefully and with a whisper of a touch, so as not to trip its wires. No one seemed to want the type of attention an explosion of that word would bring.

But there was nothing whispery about the way Tati Mimose was wielding Vodou tonight.

I took a step deeper into the living room, eager to see more. When a gruff voice rasped what sounded like "You!" I jumped like Double Dutch ropes were slapping the floor beneath my feet.

Tati Mimose waved me over.

For a moment, I considered hiding behind the wall in the hopes that my aunt would mistake what she'd seen. Being out of bed this late was not allowed. My mom liked to say, "You go looking for trouble, you gon' find it." If she and my dad found out about *this*, they would take away my tablet for the weekend, and Grandma Rose would be unbearable in her deep disappointment.

But I was too drawn in to leave now. Without realizing when or how I had come to stand before Tati Mimose, there I was. And there she was, peering down on me expectantly and mumbling words I could not make out.

"Can you repeat that, Tati?" I timidly asked. "I can't understand."

My aunt issued another throaty, unintelligible communication, gesturing in the same forceful manner that she'd warrior-danced earlier. Again, I did not comprehend a single word.

My aunt seemed so unlike herself that I wondered if Vodou's guidance and protection could be offered by an *actual* spirit who took temporary control of a person's body. That whole part? I guessed that was what put my mom and other family members off Vodou.

Tati Mimose swiped a hand into the basin again. I flinched, startled by an up-close view of the blue flames she was cupping. She then smothered the fire between her palms, rubbing briskly until I thought she'd start another fire.

A small part of me had already bolted from the room, torn down the hallway, and found a hiding place under my bed. But all the rest of me didn't budge and watched in awe as Tati Mimose, in a not-quite-herself way, laid a fire-washed hand atop the soft twists cascading from my head. I braced for a burning sensation, but instead felt a chill.

A tingly whoosh of air swept across my face, pricked my ears, and trickled along the back of my neck and down my spine. I had to wriggle a bit to let the feeling either shake off or settle in.

I inhaled sharply. My ears took in big gulps of sound, swallowing every chant, prayer, and clap-clap until all activity grew muffled for a few moments.

When my breath steadied and the sounds normalized, Tati Mimose fixed her unblinking eyes on mine and spoke again in a gravelly voice.

This time, I understood every word.

"I am the warrior from the Ogun line, here with a message for you," she began. "You have been chosen. Live in your truth."

A shiver ran through me. Gripped by a wave of fogginess, my knees buckled and I fell to the floor. And just as suddenly, I saw the light.

As in Thomas Edison's.

It was the harsh ceiling light that had been switched on, snapping Tati Mimose and me back to reality. The ceiling fan switched on, too, its whir snuffing out the prayer candles and the flame in the basin.

"What's going on here?" shrieked my mom, her astonished face in stark contrast to the image of the serene, haloed lady on her SAINT ANNE CAN tee. My wide-eyed father and my grandmother were right behind her.

The next events unfolded more quickly than I could keep up with—me clawing at the rug fibers in a feeble attempt to stand, my dad and grandma darting over to help me up, the clap-clapping women scurrying out the door, and my aunt and mom icily facing off with each other.

"Mimose, how could you?" Mom shouted, glaring at her kid sister.

As I got to my feet, I clowned, "No, no, Mom—that's actually the warrior . . . Igu, I think it was?"

My joke didn't land, which was okay. As long as it made my family see that I was unharmed and safe.

Grandma Rose's arms were outstretched, inviting me into her embrace. I rested my head on her bosom like I was doing it for her benefit, not mine.

"'You have been chosen'?" My mom echoed Tati Mimose's words. She turned to Grandma Rose. "Did you hear that, Mummy? They've cursed my baby!"

"How do you make that leap to *cursed*? Oh, right, because Vodou," Tati Mimose fired back. She snatched the basin from its perch, stormed over to a fancy laundry bag leaning against the wall, and shoved the basin in it. Next, my aunt grabbed all the cooled-down candles. Everything fit in that same bag.

Is that her Vodou travel kit? I wondered.

"Because you got my daughter mixed up in something you had no right exposing her to!" snapped Mom, stepping out of Daddy's path as he quietly set the coffee table back into its indentations on the rug.

"If I don't honor the spirits and pass what I know down to the next generation, who will?" Tati Mimose asked. She looked to Grandma Rose for backup. I saw my grandmother pinch her face, working her trademark Deep Disappointment look she'd perfected during all those decades as a high school art teacher. She said nothing.

My mom scoffed. "You have no idea what you're talking about."

Tati Mimose didn't miss a beat. "I know plenty. Including that what I did tonight is really no different from you driving hours every year to pay respect to a Catholic saint!"

Mom's eyes flashed. "Fine. For *you*. Just leave my Cicely out of it. She is to take no part in your rituals, you hear me?"

I felt the tension in my body rise. This was not good. I would do anything at that moment—belt out the *Scooby-Doo* theme song, draft a Saints & Spirits peace treaty—if I knew it would make them stop arguing. But Grandma Rose tightened her embrace around me and started to lead me away.

"All this . . . *influence*, and you use it to be selfish," my mom spat at Tati Mimose. "You will never babysit Cicely again!"

It was the last thing I heard before Grandma Rose softly closed my bedroom door behind us. She kept calm as she tucked me under my covers.

"It's all over," she assured me.

The worry in my stomach told me different. "Is it? Will they ever be friends again?"

Grandma Rose tapped my nose with her wonderfully wrinkly finger. "You've fallen out with your friend before, haven't you? I remember."

I thought about my best friend, Renee. At our last playdate, Renee had packed up her sleepover bag in a huff because I'd asked her to take a break from telling me about the news. (Renee wanted to be a journalist when she grew up, and was the only nine-year-old I knew who actually read the paper.) But we'd made up the next day.

This fight between my mom and aunt felt different.

"But Mommy and Tati Mimose are *sister* best friends."

"Well, as long as I'm around, they will stay that way."

"And after you're gone?" I asked in a little voice.

Grandma Rose smiled sadly. "I'll always be around. Even after I'm gone, you can find me in your favorite song, in the laughter of my favorite students, or . . ." Grandma Rose took off her necklace and clasped it around my neck. ". . . in the glimmer of my favorite things."

I touched the gold links around my neck.

"Understood?" asked my grandmother.

"Yes." I breathed.

I closed my eyes when I heard Grandma Rose leave the room.

I tried to return to the realm I was in before—the one with the shooting stars. But I was too weighed down by worries to travel the cosmos now.

What had happened at the ceremony tonight? Was my mom right? Had I been cursed?

I kept hearing my mom's other words play in my head.

You will never babysit Cicely again!

How could I reach for the stars when one of the biggest in the galaxy—Tati Mimose—had been declared off-limits to me?

My universe wouldn't be the same without her.

CHAPTER ONE

Present Day

I must be cursed.

Maybe it's just bad luck, but beginnings always seem to go wrong for me. And the way something kicks off determines how it lands, right?

Today, the Thursday before Labor Day, is my first day of sophomore year—and I'm running late. I rush through the doors of Christian Prep, weaving through the hallway mob like I'm swimming upstream.

Last night I did everything right: I set positive intentions while ironing and laying out my uniform, took a bath with the healing salts Tati Mimose posted about on her socials . . . and I *still* overslept! All that needs to happen now for me to *truly* be on brand is to get lost on the way to class.

I speed-snake my way through chatty Black and Brown students in white polos with starched collars, smooth khakis, pleated gray skirts, and maroon sweaters. Everyone's braids, twists, 'fros, locs, coils, curls, edges, or straight strands are first-day fresh. Everyone has that prayed-over sheen to them. I breathe in a mix of scented lotion and that fresh-out-the-box-school-supplies smell.

Things could be worse. On the first day of my freshman year, I got hit by a parked car.

That's word!

As I stepped off a curb between two seemingly parked cars, the quiet hybrid crept back and bumped my leg. The car stopped as soon as I slapped my palm against its trunk, and it did no more than ashen up my skin, but still.

And let's not relive my cringey first day of eighth grade. Long story, but it involved a crowded after-school meetup, a super-clear glass wall, and my forehead. *Konk!*

Finally, out of breath, I make it to my first-period class, World Literature. It's only ten seconds after the late bell.

"Always one straggler in every bunch," the teacher, Sister Lucille, snarks dryly.

I ignore the muffled chuckles around me. Winded, I plop into the first empty desk I find.

Why would a teacher give anyone a hard time for dragging a little this morning? Most of us have barely had time to adjust to this new and early start date. It's still August, for Beyoncé's sake! True, I have cousins in Atlanta who start school in damn near July, but this is Brooklyn.

In Brooklyn, it's still very much summer. Every breathing West Indian around here knows that our version of Caribbean

Carnival—the much-anticipated event also known as the West Indian Day Parade, or the Labor Day Parade—marks the official end of summer break. The parade is happening this coming Monday.

It's tradition.

And this year? The parade also falls on my birthday. That feels like a little bit of the good luck I need.

Sister Lucille begins to take attendance. I raise my hand when she calls my name, then sneak a glance down at my phone in my lap. I know I'll have to stash it away before class starts for real, but I can't resist checking out my aunt's latest post.

It's a selfie that shows off Mimose's stunning features. She's got her coils gorgeously pinned into those classic 1940s hair rolls. Tati Mimose and I have the same dark chestnut tresses, brown eyes, and heart-shaped brown face. But when I once tried to copy that same retro hairstyle, I looked like one of those pastoral sheep with spiral horns.

I notice an altar set up behind my aunt. It's lined with tall prayer candles, dried flowers, and tiny framed photos of ancestors who are no longer with us. My eyes sting when they land on Grandma Rose's photo.

My everything, Grandma Rose, passed away last year. (The rest of my freshman year did not get much better after I got hit by that parked car.)

Grandma Rose not being here for my birthday feels unbearable. What will it be like, not waking up on Monday to her rendition of "Bon Anniversaire," the old-time French "Happy Birthday" song she'd learned from her own grandmother?

My breathing quickens and sweat pricks at my temples at the thought of not hearing Grandma Rose's painfully off-key vocals. She sounded like an electric guitar with strep throat and it made my ears want to weep. I used to troll her about her singing, but now I just miss it.

To keep from drowning in a swell of sadness, I laser-focus on the caption underneath my aunt's photo:

Wanna know something SENSATIONAL? Carnival is gonna hit different this year.

I feel a tingle of intrigue, grateful for the distraction. I wonder what my aunt's mystery caption means?

The post already has thousands of likes. My aunt is a Vodouista influencer—though the Vodou she presents on her social media is more like a fusion of New Age rituals mixed with island dabbling. Tati Mimose is a Brooklyn-born-and-bred Haitian like both my parents, so she takes creative license with her spirituality. She wears her beliefs on her ethically made sleeves, and her followers praise her for it. Some people follow her for her tarot card readings and aesthetically pleasing posts. Others like how she reps the culture, no filter. Or they just dig her because she's hella beautiful.

I follow her because I don't get to see her that often in real life. Ever since the blowout fight they had when I was nine, the tension between my aunt and my mom has been a few city blocks thick. But at least we always had Grandma Rose, the bridge that

14

kept Mom and Tati Mimose connected and together. Ever since my grandma passed, that bridge has been burned, and the rift between my aunt and mom has gotten even wider.

I double-tap my aunt's post to like it, but instead I unmute the sound.

Papash's "Sensational" thumps from my phone speakers.

"Aaaaye," someone shouts.

"Labor Day a'comin'!" someone else trumpets in proud patois.

From the second the beat drops, the class is instantly hype. They can't even help it. Heads start bobbing and voices call out the lyrics. This time of year, it takes nothing to get people jumping up to jump-ups.

A Papash bop is especially welcome. Papash is an island bredren, from Brooklyn, and, in my opinion, the illest rapper today. (Oh, and he's gorgeous.) Listening to his music has been my escape lately. There's something about the notes in his voice that ring true. And all of Flatbush lost their minds when he released "Sensational," a Carnival-themed banger earlier this summer to rep Caribbean hoods like ours. It's expected to be the biggest song at Carnival. But my DJ slipup is causing a stir at the wrong time.

"Where is that coming from?" demands Sister Lucille.

Frantic, I tap my screen to silence the song, but that only makes the music stop and start again. I scroll up, but that triggers the sound on the next post, some sort of movie trailer.

"Who played that music?" Sister Lucille asks, looking every

bit like Harriet the Spy in a nun cap. She starts making her way down the aisle in her chunky orthopedic shoes.

Oh no.

I manage to close out of the app, then reach an arm back to slip my phone into the unzipped pocket of my bag.

One person takes notice of my movements—the boy sitting across from me. Roll call refreshed my memory of his name: Kwame Hilliard.

He watches me with interest, like he's piecing things together. A throat-click sound that could either be a snort of laughter or a sneeze escapes him. I look over and his eyes meet mine like it's his gotcha moment.

He *could* snitch. One thing I didn't enjoy about my honors classes freshman year was the competitiveness that made everything feel a little like *The Hunger Games*. But Kwame Hilliard is a new face in the honors group. I'd seen him in passing last year—a blink of his piled-high 'fro bobbing down the halls, or a flash of his smile in the cafeteria line—but that's about it. I don't really know him, though I have noticed he's got a lot of friends. Now I'm noticing a few more things about him—like the fact that he's observant, which is a church usher's way of saying nosy.

"God bless you," I respond to his sneezy throat click, meeting his eyes as if daring him to tell on me.

A slow smirk tugs one corner of his mouth. "Thank you," he answers, signing this moment's contract to confirm that, yes, he'll keep my secret.

"You're welcome" is my thank-you to him.

He nods, amused.

Even though I'm finished with my phone, my phone isn't finished with me. Just as Sister Lucille walks by my desk, it buzzes like a rat-sized bee in my bag. I sit very still, my heart galloping. That's gotta be my bestie, Renee. She texts me with breaking news, no matter when she comes across it—even in the middle of her Latin class.

I hold my breath as Sister Lucille stops behind me. In my efforts to look as casual as possible, I come short of whistling a jaunty showtune.

As soon as Sister Lucille turns to go, I reach back to switch off my phone. I can't chance any more slipups. The moment my fingers don't feel the familiar ridges of my galaxy-print case, I panic.

"Looking for this?" Sister Lucille asks, my phone gleaming as she sways it side to side.

Sister Sticky Fingaz? The former tween magician in me would *almost* be impressed by her sleight of hand—if I weren't mortified.

And speaking of hands, mine are still frozen on my backpack, because apparently I can't move and think of a good lie at the same time. "Uh, I was just grabbing . . . something."

Sister Lucille looks down at my phone screen and reads Renee's text out loud:

"'Yo, your aunt is a goddess. Did you see her post? What's that all about?'"

The entire class erupts in volcanic laughter and my cheeks start burning like hot lava.

Most kids don't know my aunt is the famed influencer Mimose Benoirs. If they know anything about me, it's that my parents run the struggling Haitian take-out restaurant Port-au-Princesse.

And now, apparently, that I'm the object of Sister Lucille's comedy routine.

"Whew, now *I* want to see this post," Sister Lucille sighs, faux impressed. One of her hands is holding my phone and the other is fanning the air. The way she's performing, you'd think there's a NUN' BUT LAUGHS sign over a velvet rope outside the classroom and we all paid a cover charge to get in here.

Chuckles break out once again, and I note how little it takes for reasonable people to act like a stale laugh track.

I glance sideways and see that Kwame is still watching me with a hitch of his eyebrow. I boldly meet his watchful stare. Now the amusement—or relief?—quirking one corner of his mouth communicates something different: I am of some comfort to him. Maybe he thought class with honors nerds would be robotic. I'm not sure he expected there'd be any humans malfunctioning, and I can tell this relaxes him.

In this moment, him and me, eye to eye, we are the reverse Adam and Eve, aware of our nakedness but not hiding it from each other. We don't run for cover. We don't place a fig leaf over what lies exposed: His honors class discomfort. My chaotic moment. Understanding this, and seeing my faults welcomed, relaxes *me*. For a minute, anyway.

"I will hold on to your phone until the end of class, Ms. Destin," Sister Lucille tells me sharply. She turns on her Boomer heels and begins her slow creep to the front of the classroom.

"Speaking of goddesses," my teacher continues as I slump in my seat. "Which Greek-mythology goddess could be considered the patron saint of popularity? Anyone want to take a guess?"

Kwame starts fidgeting like a *Jeopardy* contestant with a broken buzzer. He knows the answer. But he's scanning the room as if expecting someone else to respond. Why doesn't he just say it? I raise my eyebrows and give him a look like, *Speak up*.

Kwame's ink-black eyes shift to me and he mumbles, "Pheme," under his breath as if expecting me to share. Um, not gonna happen. I'm trying to stay unseen right now.

"Did somebody say Pheme?" questions Sister Lucille, glancing toward our corner of the classroom. "I thought I just heard the answer come from this area. No?"

Kwame doesn't own up to it.

"Must've been my imagination," she relents. "But Pheme is right. Known as the goddess of popularity, Pheme would go viral pretty regularly if she were a real person in today's world."

I give Kwame a knowing look, which he acknowledges with a wink. I roll my eyes and look away, fighting back a smile. At least I can feel some of the awkwardness of being put on blast melt away.

For the rest of the class, Sister Lucille has us read and discuss a passage in our *Mythology Through the Ages* book. When the bell rings and I stand up, she walks over and hands me my phone.

"This isn't freshman year anymore," she says quietly. "We're stepping things up. Phones off in my class."

Chastened, I nod and inch my way into the bottlenecking crowd heading out the door.

In the hallway, friends separated during class reunite like matching pairs of socks after a tumble in the dryer. I feel a pang of sadness that Renee and I have totally opposite schedules this year that keep us from seeing each other during the day—another bit of bad luck. But I'm happy that we'll be meeting up after school to go shopping for Carnival outfits.

"Sister Lucille may be getting old, but nothing wrong with her hearing."

It's Kwame, who is suddenly beside me. I meet the challenge that sparkles in his eyes.

"She could hear your phone buzzing a mile away," he adds.

How dare he bring that up?

"Not as clearly as she heard your nerdy answer," I bite back. When he looks around to make sure no one else heard me, I can't help but smirk.

He nods. "Okay, I see how it's gonna be."

"Yo, Professor Kwame!" his friends call out, slapping his back as we merge into the hallway traffic.

"He don't even look the same," another friend jokes. "My dude, why is your 'fro like a whole inch shorter?"

As they lead him down the corridor, Kwame manages to communicate one last thing to me—the slightest hint of a shoulder shrug that seems to sign off from the Kwame I met in class to another, more Pheme-ous Kwame.

I get it.

Mind swirling, I head toward my second-period class . . . in the wrong direction. Of course.

I spin my behind around to go the right way, and tell myself this flustered feeling is because sophomore is off to a rocky start. It has nothing at all to do with Kwame Hilliard.

CHAPTER TWO

"You know Sister Lucille was just messing with you," Renee says, and deftly sucks her teeth as we step outside school. "And nobody's thinking about your cafeteria mustard spill. Trust. If you ask me, the stain kinda looks cute. Like a 'C' monogram."

I look down at the splotch of yellow on my white polo shirt, courtesy of a slipup I had with the mustard squeeze bottle at lunch. I shake my head. "Not seeing it, but okay."

As my best friend and I walk down the street, I can't shake the feeling that I really might be cursed. Logically, I know a bad first day of school doesn't mean I'm in for a bad year. So why is Doubt shredding that argument like its street name is Edward Scissorhands?

I guess I'll just have to see which way this year will go.

The thought hits me as Renee and I are literally standing at a crossroads. This is the Junction, the huge intersection in our neighborhood where island culture blooms and coils itself around everything. Here you'll find plentiful plantains at the bodega, and peppery patois on every tongue. It's kind of like the Times Square of Flatbush: a destination throbbing with businesses of all kinds—big box, mom-and-pop, street vendors—plus the people they attract, most of them speaking in English or French-based Creole.

We longtime locals know these streets so well, we can recognize every ancient blot of sidewalk chewing gum. Newcomers, though, love that the Junction is accessible to Manhattan, thanks to the train line right at the cross streets of Nostrand and Flatbush Avenues.

Renee and I expertly outpace the stampede of the subway commuters emerging from below, their eyes squinting in the light. I can almost sense their inner compasses recalibrating as they orient themselves to life aboveground.

It's somehow on me to make sure Renee doesn't collide with anyone. The girl insists on keeping her brown eyes locked on her phone as she walks. She's afraid to miss any piece of potential news.

"Gangway!" I warn, but all she does is laugh at my old-timey slang that I picked up watching TV classics with Grandma Rose.

We join a small crowd of people at the corner waiting for the light, and I look around.

It's one thing to be alive in these Brooklyn streets. But Brooklyn streets during Carnival season are another dimension entirely. It's a wonder the curbside vendors have any island nation flags left.

Every car that drives past has their homeland flag flapping hello. Having lived here our whole lives, Renee and I recognize each one we spot—Guyana, Saint Kitts and Nevis, Jamaica, Barbados, Haiti, Trinidad and Tobago, Saint Vincent and the Grenadines, Bahamas, Saint Lucia, Panama, Antigua, Grenada, Dominica, Montserrat, Turks and Caicos, Suriname, Belize, Puerto Rico, the Dominican Republic, Cuba, the Cayman Islands, all the Virgin Islands. Everyone is ready to represent.

Renee looks up from her phone to take in my still-tense expression. She reaches up to my shoulder and affectionately tugs one of my twists.

"You good?" she rasps. Renee has the best voice—husky and strong. Even though she's petite—a full head and a half shorter than me—her voice is tall enough to dunk on any baller at Barclays Center.

"I am," I say, trying to shake off my worry cloud.

"Promise?" Renee says.

"Promise," I say. She lifts her pinky and I hook mine around hers, sealing the "we got this" pact we've perfected ever since the fourth grade, when we mutually agreed to do life as besties. My bony brown pinky entwined with her plump brown one is familiar as ever.

As we cross the street, Renee glances back at her phone and gasps. "Okay, ready for this?" she asks me.

Informing people is Renee's *thing*. It drives her. And I admire her whole journalistic heart. She works hard constantly updating her heinous-crime-breaking-news Twitter account, @Isitoneofus. It's gaining in popularity as more Black folks follow her to find out whether or not a suspect behind a viral incident is Black. People appreciate it for the sweet relief or the shared embarrassment space it offers.

"What is it?" I ask, bracing myself for more potentially bad news.

But Renee is smiling. She pulls me over to stand in the cool shade below the awning of West Indian Village Accounting, LLC. She switches her bag to the opposite shoulder and smooths her already-slicked-down side ponytail with one hand.

"You'll never guess," she begins.

I'm reminded of how much Grandma Rose loved my Breaking-News Renee impersonations, and a quick sorrow tugs at my heart. I would run through all of Renee's story setups, from "Did you hear" to "You'll never guess." When Renee would skip the suspense, it was only with a terse "Girl," "Sis," and my personal preference: "Yooooo."

In those moments, Grandma Rose marveled at how much I moved and even sounded like Renee. "How do you do that?" she'd ask, laughing. "It's like you really jumped right *into* Renee's spirit and started wearing it around."

Grandma Rose's comment stayed with me. I got chills once when I read that the Latin root words in *impersonate* are "into" and "a person"—which, to me, sounds real shape-shifty. Are we dipping into another person's essence on some level when we impersonate them so well?

Renee gives my arm a squeeze. "Cicely, you with me?"

I blink away my memories and smile. "The suspense is killing me, girl. Out with it!" I shout playfully.

Renee beams under the rays of my full attention.

"You wouldn't *believe*," she says. "Papash is performing at the parade!"

She can barely get out the last few words before I start jumping up and down. "Ohmygodnoway!" I screech. "Wait. How do you know? Are you sure?"

Renee has already anticipated this question, because she's holding out her screen to me.

I sigh at the photo of silky-skinned Papash on a rooftop, holding out his arms as if he's giving Brooklyn a hug. The boy looks exquisite in his simple white tee and jeans that show off his sculpted, rice-and-peas-fed physique. But Papash is more than a beautiful face fronting a dope beat. He's a nineteen-year-old peacemaker. The only thing more amazing than his message of unity and love is his voice. I'm convinced his vocals are on some healing frequency, because I feel lighter after hearing him. After Grandma Rose's funeral, I listened to his studio album and live performances nonstop on Spotify. It . . . helped.

"He just posted the news on his IG," Renee says, pointing to the caption. "He says that before his performance, he'll be a guest on a podcast that's recording live at the parade. And yo—a local Haitian American influencer is going to interview him!"

My heart jumps for a second. *A local Haitian American*

26

influencer? I think of my aunt, and her cryptic post with the Papash music from this morning. Was that meant to be a hint? Could it be . . . ?

"Are you thinking what I'm thinking?" Renee asks, her eyes sparkling.

I am, but I don't want to get my hopes up. "The host is probably a historian," I say, "or a DJ, or a costume designer . . ."

"Maybe," Renee says. "But Mimose has over two hundred thousand followers. Celebrities are starting to consult her, and her sponsors are only getting bigger."

"Should I call her to find out?" I ask, unsure. "Or maybe text?"

This is embarrassing. I'm so out of touch with my own aunt that I'm craving Renee's advice on something I should know the answer to.

"I'll just text her a quick hello," I say as confidently as I can. "Good idea . . . right?"

Renee backs me up with a nod. "Please tell her hello for me. And that I hope to see her *soon*," she adds with a wink.

"I got you," I say, editing my intro to include my bestie.

Hello from me and Renee! How are you? I saw your IG post and am here to say, SAAAME. I'm excited Carnival lands on my bday this year. And you heard Papash is expected to perform?!? Hope to see you on de Parkway! Miss u!

27

There. It's done.

Renee and I start walking again, and I keep my phone in hand, awaiting my aunt's response.

"Can you imagine if Mimose really is the person who'll be interviewing Papash?" Renee says. "And then maybe *we'd* get a chance to meet him? I would levitate."

Well, yes, why not dream big? If my aunt is interviewing Papash, maybe she'd invite me along. That would be the best fifteenth-birthday gift I could ever imagine.

"Anything can happen on Labor Day weekend," I say, feeling suddenly hopeful.

We step onto a sidewalk grate just as an arriving subway sends up a whoosh of warm air. Our flyaway strands flutter, giving a hint of prophecy to my words.

Renee smooths down her hair and harrumphs. "Yeah, that's what my granny says after watching the five o'clock news."

"I don't mean it that way. You're Trini," I say, because respect due to Trinidad and Tobago, which throws the biggest carnival in all of the Caribbean. "You know it's the happiest time of the year for these streets. Plus, I don't remember the last time my birthday fell on Labor Day. It's like Caribbean Christmas."

No sooner do I make my declaration than my phone buzzes with a call. I check the screen.

"It's my aunt!" I get all wiggly, especially in the legs.

"Stop all that dancing and answer it, yo!"

"Tati Mimose, hi!" I singsong in greeting, and Renee waves her arms like an orchestral conductor.

Normally, it would annoy me to no end if an adult responded to my text with a call, but I couldn't be happier right now. I can hardly talk for smiling so hard. I've missed my aunt, and haven't seen her in ages. This past summer, she texted me invites to some of her rooftop gatherings, but my mom would always remark on how distasteful it was for Mimose to be hosting parties so soon after their mom's death.

"Hey, girlie!" says my aunt. "You know I must have too much going on when I forget to plan something for your birthday. It completely slipped my mind until your text reminded me."

It's true. My aunt is big on birthdays. For my fourteenth, she threw a rooftop party in my honor. I cherish that memory even more now, knowing that was the last time Grandma Rose would celebrate anything with us. Her breast cancer returned with a vengeance three months later, and she never recovered.

I press my cell closer to my clammy ear. "Oh, no worries, Tati. You have more than earned a year off birthday duty."

My aunt scoffs. "It's a pleasure, never a duty, Cicely."

"Aw, thanks for saying that," I say, catching Renee's wrap-up-the-small-talk-and-get-to-the-point arm roll. "You say you've been busy. Whatchu working on now?"

Renee emphatically thumbs-ups me.

"Funny you ask, because I just thought of a way to make up for my birthday blunder."

My knees buckle and Renee catches me just in time. "I'm listening," I manage to say through labored breathing.

"How would you like to meet Papash on Monday?"

A scream of pure joy rises from my throat. I'm sure I'm radiating ultraviolet beams of euphoria from my pores because Renee is squinting so hard right now.

Tati Mimose laughs her signature cackle. "I'll take that as a yes."

"Ohmygodthankyou!" I sputter. "Are you the one who's interviewing him, then?"

"I am," Tati Mimose says proudly. "For the *Soundstage* podcast. So I'm supposed to meet him before his performance at the parade. And you can join me!"

Wow. Talk about my luck turning.

Renee starts pointing at herself like she's poking holes in her aura.

"Oh, oh, and my best friend, Renee?" I ask. "Could she come meet him, too?"

"I'll put her down as my plus-one's plus-one!" Tati Mimose answers from the depths of her generous heart. "The only thing is, I have a client meeting early that morning. You can come along to that—it'll just be a quick reading—and then we'll scoop up your friend and go meet Papash."

"Of course! Anything, I'm there!" I bubble over. A part of me is excited to check out this reading. My aunt knows of my secret fascination with all things spiritual. Now and then I'll pop in to watch her IG Live readings. This is the first in-person one I'll be attending—at least since I observed that ceremony in my house when I was nine. But my aunt and I never talk about that night.

I thank Tati Mimose again and end the call. My world feels like it's expanded three times its size. Renee's eyes dart back and forth, like she's already crafting the perfect parade updates for her followers.

I throw up my arms and jog in place, nearly taking a high knee to my chin. "We'regonnameetPapash!"

Renee shuts her eyes and opens her mouth wide. When she finally makes a sound, it's to chant along with me: "We'regonnameetPapash! We'regonnameetPapash!"

There's only so much jumping you can do wearing polyester uniforms in this heat, so we quit it and catch our breaths. And then I catch sight of my mustard monogram *C* on my polo shirt. Is it me, or has the stain started to fade a bit?

"A do-over!" I announce. "Today might have been a trash first day, but now I get a do-over."

My best friend's eyes widen. "Does your aunt have some sort of Sankofa time-travel portal? If she does, I promise I will not so much as journal about it."

I bunch up my lips and look at her sideways. Renee laughs and shuffles out of my reach.

"Not a *literal* do-over," I explain. "Just a chance to start again, fresh. My birthday is like my personal start to a new year, right? And the Labor Day Parade is everyone else's, so that's double the win right there. Caribbean Christmas!"

"Aay, aay!" Renee hypes me on in time to the soca song blaring from a passing car.

My best friend and I turn and walk down the street, arm in arm. I catch our reflections in a store window and do a little strut. In our gray pleated uniform skirts and tall socks, I feel a little bit like we're Cher and Dionne in *Clueless*.

"This is fifteen," I announce.

"Technically," teases Renee, "you're fourteen point nine years old."

I scrunch up my nose. "Just admit you're excited we'll be the same age again."

"You do realize that fifteen is a big deal," Renee says as we cross the street.

"I know—the year before sweet sixteen."

"It's not that. Statistically, it's the age most American kids get their first kiss!"

My eyebrows jump in the split second it takes for Kwame's face to flash in my mind. Without realizing it, I exhale.

Renee playfully nudges my shoulder. "I saw that. Who were you just thinking about?"

I can't hide anything from this girl. She's like an info bloodhound, and once she's picked up on a scent, she can't help but follow it. Anyway, I have no desire to hide anything from Renee. I trust her more than anyone.

"This boy in my World Lit class," I whisper, coming to a stop and making sure no one from school happens to be walking past us. "Kwame."

"Which one is he?"

"The one with the 'fro who's always got this easy pace."

"Xavier? Ooh, he's the cutest boy at school!"

"No, Xavier has the curly dark 'fro. Kwame's 'fro is more coily brown."

"You sure he's not a junior?"

I go on my phone and show Renee Kwame's IG. His latest post is a pic of him standing outside his centrally located apartment building with the caption *Best seat in the house for parade viewing!*

Renee's smile stretches ear to ear. "Oh, *that* guy. He's cute."

Our thirst taps out when a text comes through from my mom. *Adeline has done it again.*

My mom's sent me a photo of a tasty Haitian dish: lambi, otherwise known as conch.

Adeline is the new cook my parents hired for their restaurant after Mom's fusion dishes weren't selling. Adeline is an OG Haitian and her bomb recipes are straight from the island, unaltered. Port-au-Princesse gets a redo of sorts, too, I realize. For the first time, my parents will be vendors at the parade, so it's a huge opportunity to reach new customers.

"Yo, tell your mom she should post that online," says Renee.

My mom has no clout. For some reason, she just can't get people to follow her—on social media or in life.

I shrug. "She'll post something and barely get three likes. Now with Grandma Rose gone, that's down to two likes."

"Maybe she just believes that the best advertisement is good product," Renee says as we start walking again.

"I agree with her on that, but she could do better with spreading the word." I sigh.

Even with Adeline, business at Port-au-Princesse hasn't been great. The only people who know about the restaurant seem to be broke high school students, because my softhearted mom lets them hang out there without ordering much.

"I like talking to your mom," Renee says. "She's the one who taught me the difference between jam and jelly."

"See what I mean? Not exactly edgy or earth-shattering stuff." I pause, then add, "The best thing would be to have Mimose promote Port-au-Princesse on *her* account. All Mom has to do is ask my aunt, but she never will."

"Is it a pride thing?"

I shrug again. "Probably. It's just—ever since Grandma Rose passed, I feel like I've become the rope in their tug-of-war. Lately, I've had to kinda hide when I go see my aunt and it's . . . awkward."

"Would your mom get salty if she knew about Monday?" Renee asks with a small frown.

"She would act like she's not, but I'd know different. And I don't want to make things worse between them. So I think I'll keep everything on the low. It's better that way."

Renee nods like she gets it.

"But," I add, feeling a burst of excitement, "I can't worry about their nonsense now."

Without even having to discuss it, we know we are on a mission. A fashion mission. If we're meeting Papash on Monday, we have to look the part.

"We're going for folklore meets function," says Renee. "That's our motivation."

I don't know exactly what she means by "folklore meets function," but I trust the confident look on her face. When we tell the epic story of sophomore-year Carnival, our outfits will have a place in that canon.

We walk by the big-box stores where we shopped for swimsuits at the start of summer, and head for the tried-and-true small businesses that have been there since we were toddlers. The small business owners, who hail from all corners of the globe, are the same people we grew up watching our grandmothers haggle with. We don't bat an eye when these shop owners greet our aunties and uncles in Haitian, Trinidadian, or Jamaican Creole. Some of them have family who have married into the Caribbean community. They literally make it their business to know us. So we know they have the inventory that people around here are looking for. Especially at this time of year.

Renee and I lock eyes on the same storefront window sign that reads LABOR DAY SALE. We make a beeline for the boutique.

But then we hear an adult call to us. Our instincts pick up on that unmistakable beckoning, similar to when a relative calls you to find the remote or fetch a glass of water.

"Little Cindy! Little Cindy daugh-tah!" An older man's raspy voice rings out with a Trini accent.

Renee stops short and glances over at the man who's calling out her great-grandmother Miss Cindy's name in these streets. He's standing outside a storefront that has a poster in its window that reads COSTUMING THE LABOR DAY PARADE SINCE 1967. From the looks of the Carnival-costumed mannequins and steel drums inside, this space has been converted into a mas camp: headquarters for all the costume-making and prepping for a particular masquerade troupe. Dope.

"How are you, Uncle?" Renee asks the older man as we approach him.

I can tell she knows him but has no idea what his name is.

I'm getting an unmistakable I've-been-to-your-baptism vibe from him. He smiles and a gold tooth gleams in the late-day sun. He has a gray beard and thick crown of locs, and he's wearing a T-shirt with the words BOTANY BAE across the front. I wonder what that is. He seems too old to even know about the word *bae*.

"Are you ready for the parade?" he asks like he's the proud papa of Brooklyn itself.

"Yes, I can't wait." Renee nods politely. "It's going to be fun."

The lines on his forehead deepen, and his beard vibrates when he says, "It's not just fun. It's a celebration."

"A celebration, yes. That's what I meant."

The man stretches out his arms the way Papash did in that rooftop pic. "Carnival shows the world that we survived." He smiles and shows the sun a twinning golden tooth. "Our Africanness not only survived but is thriving."

I've never heard the parade described this way.

"Yes, it's merged with the ways of Westerners," the man goes on, "but with a vibrant, soulful twist. So, soak it all in—the costumes, the music, the fellowship, the *food*. Let it all feed you."

"Yes, sir," I say with a smile. I can't help but be charmed by this elder. It's like he's found a way to bottle up the pre-parade vibes and give people sips from it in conversation.

A sudden look of caution seizes his face. "I know you're not going to go to J'Ouvert. You don't want to get mixed up with the element there. Stay far away," he warns.

We both nod. "We will," answers Renee.

J'Ouvert is the more macabre pre-parade celebration that takes place in another part of Brooklyn the night before. I've always been curious about it, but I've never been allowed to go. It's a shame how this darker, spookier version of Carnival has become a magnet for criminal activity.

"Our people are hurting and fighting and killing each other for nonsense, using this time to settle scores over nothing." The man shakes his head. "I'll be at J'Ouvert because my pan band plays there, but I've got the shield of my ancestors to protect me."

Renee and I nod empathetically. His talk of ancestors reminds me of Tati Mimose, who I know lights candles for select people who once walked the earth. She's always quick to point out that Catholic saints are ancestors, too, yet somehow it's not considered taboo to honor and ask *them* for guidance.

"I've been trying to ring your grandmother," the man tells Renee. "She's not been picking up."

"Okay, I'll let her know."

"You'll let her know what."

"That you've been calling."

"That who been calling?"

Uh-oh, now Renee is in trouble, because it's clear she has no idea what his name is. My eyes dart from the elder to my best friend.

"Tell her Uncle Rufus has been calling her," the man finally says, letting Renee off the hook. Whew.

"How about I text her now?" offers Renee.

As she takes out her phone, Uncle Rufus turns his attention to me. "And you there. Where your people from?"

"Haiti," I tell him.

"Oh, Haiti. I bet you know the exact year of their revolutionary victory. I never met a Haitian who didn't."

"1804," I say with a smile.

"There it is." He nods, chuckling. "Your people have a fierce spirit and a resilient one as well. But we can't forget the first to gain their independence, even before Haiti. Have you ever heard of the Black people in Colombia who formed their own independent village in the late 1600s?"

"No, I never heard of them," I admit, making a mental note to look this up later. Maybe *independent* means they do carnival on a huge scale. Or maybe it simply means they get to practice whatever spiritual traditions their people have been practicing for eons.

"One blood. One people. Many flavors. And what we do here on this soil, jubilating as we do, only lifts up the vibes of this entire city."

"Yes," I answer, dazzled by the pageantry of his professorial street lecture.

"I tell you, bredren, the streets may not be full up of the tropical flora we left behind in the islands," Uncle Rufus says, gesturing to passersby. "But look at the flowers, look at the strong trees, look how deep the roots go."

"That's right," says a man who sits on a milk crate he's just carried out of a nearby shop.

"True, true," says his companion.

"So, I'm glad to be alive," Uncle Rufus concludes. "Wherever you all are, I'm reminded of home. I hope to see you having a good, safe time at the parade. And you tell your grandmother we're waiting for her today."

Renee and I nod politely and then rush off to the shop. Anyone who wants our attention between here and there, we'll pretend not to hear them. Even if it's the ancestors calling us.

Our fashionable ancestors, though, are speaking to us today. In no time at all, Renee and I are behind a fitting room curtain editing our haul. We've gathered shoes, rompers, skorts, and even a couple of flags for good measure.

But the most amazing finds are these off-the-shoulder ruffle tops that look like they were cut from the folk dresses that island cultural dancers wear. Someone came up with the brilliant idea to remix these tops and add flag colors. Somebody local had to have designed them.

The Haiti one is satiny, with a swirly trim along the ruffled top. Trinidad and Tobago's has the same look, but with a T&T flag. When we try them on, they fit beautifully.

"These are perfect for Monday," I say, regarding our reflections in the mirror. I can't believe we're actually going to meet Papash. And that I'll finally get to spend time with my aunt.

"It's a celebration," Renee intones in Uncle Rufus's voice.

I snatch my Haiti flag off our haul pile and hand Renee the Trinidad and Tobago flag.

"Grab something and wave! Grab something and wave!" We sing the classic Carnival hype song and dance in the cramped space.

Caribbean Christmas, here we come!

CHAPTER THREE

"'Twas the night before Carnival and all through the hood, every-thing was stirring, everybody felt good," I freestyle to an audience of none as soon as I step into my lamplit bedroom.

It's way past midnight and I'm exhausted. But my Papash-fueled anticipation keeps me in a bars-spitting mood.

"My outfit was hung by my window with care, in hopes that Caribbean Christmas soon would be there," I add with a groggy smile.

I drop onto my bed, sinking my head deeper into my pillow. And then I snap out of it.

I gotta set my alarm!

I fish my phone out the back pocket of my pajama shorts and also pull out a folded sticky note. I'd forgotten that I wrote down my dad's quote about my mom. He said it a few hours ago when we were in the kitchen prepping food for tomorrow. Mom and I shook our heads and chuckled at the time, but that was because of the goofy way he said it. The fact is, his statement was more sweet than funny.

Nothing she does surprises me, but everything she does impresses me.

"That's a good one," I whisper.

I've had this habit since I was a kid—jotting down quotes or thoughts on scraps of paper. I've got notes all over my bedroom—on my dresser, on my desk, on a corkboard above my desk, on my bedside table pinned under hematite stones. I reach over and place this latest note under a smooth black crystal. A scatter of notes here, a pile of clothes there. My room is getting to be such a mess.

My plan was to break open my new brush pens at some point and turn the quotes into wall art. I could curate and frame all the notes on the wall above my desk. Dollar-store frames would be so easy to get, though I have yet to buy them. I heave out a sigh and bookmark this internal lecture for another day.

I set my alarm for 6:00 a.m., put my phone on my nightstand, and flop back onto my pillow.

I think back over the past couple of days. Late into the muggy nights, street curbs, brownstone stoops, and apartments were lit and at capacity, everyone liming to the soundtrack of their choice, from reggae music to howling laughter to somebody's stovetop pan of sizzling grease.

The weekend before Carnival is usually a sleepless one. It's like the movie trailer before the blockbuster that promises to make the pavement quake come Monday. Right now, my

Brooklyn neighborhood is the propped-open eyelids of the city that doesn't sleep.

Normally on Labor Day weekend, Renee comes over, my cousins from Jersey are in town, and we all hang out at my place. The adults don't even mind how loud we bump our music, because on Carnival weekend, anything goes. We generally end up sleeping in the living room after staying up late listening to music, watching movies, and eating beef patties.

This weekend, though, has been different. My parents will be vendors at the parade, so we were so busy prepping that we didn't have time for guests. When I wasn't chopping bell peppers and onions, I was hand-lettering and printing mini leaflets advertising their location along the parade route. The only person we had over on Sunday night was the Port-au-Princesse cook, Adeline. She and my parents prepared the meats in our kitchen—choice beef cuts, chicken wings and thighs, and delicious pork cubes— and listened to a retro Carnival playlist of all the classics my family raised me on. There were stacks of aluminum pans and disposable plates and cups on every available counter space. Buckets of meat lined the floors, and herbs, spices, and produce were piled on top of the kitchen table.

In bed now, I toss and turn. I'm a bundle of nerves and excitement about the fact that I'll be seeing my aunt—and meeting Papash—tomorrow. Well, technically today. Which means it's technically already my birthday.

I feel like a little kid, and I remember that long-ago sensation of soaring through the stars. The memory relaxes me, and I drift right to the edge of sleep, where reality plays with dreamworld.

Then I hear echoes of a faint voice mingling with the street sounds outside my window. It sounds like my grandmother softly singing "Bon Anniversaire."

And the thing is, it doesn't feel out of the ordinary. Neither does the scent of Grandma Rose's perfume tickling my nose.

"Thank you, Grandma," I croak against my pillow, way too drowsy and comfy to question it, or lift my head, or open my eyes. I keep them closed and focus on an image of candles glowing on top of a cake. Is that Grandma holding the cake? The waves of heat from the flames are blurring out the face.

"My birthday wish is to spend this day with you," I sigh.

The sudden feeling of a soft summer breeze tickling my face is the last thing I remember.

When my alarm goes off at 6:00 a.m., I sit up with more energy than I should have after sleeping about four hours. That's gotta be a good sign.

And it really does feel like Christmas morning. I practically jump out of bed and look out my bedroom window, half expecting to hear sleigh bells.

Instead, I hear music. *Slay bells?* Stevie Wonder's "Happy Birthday" is playing on a loop, and when I swing open my bedroom door, the sound confetti hits me. I realize my parents are playing the music downstairs.

My mom meets me at the bottom of the carpeted stairs with

her arms outstretched for a hug. "There's the birthday girl!"

She's already fully dressed in her PORT-AU-PRINCESSE tee, her curly 'fro accented with pretty beaded HAITI hair combs. There's enough love in her brown eyes and honey-coated voice to fill in all the Grandma-Rose-and-Tati-Mimose-sized gaps in this moment. I just don't understand why she's making it so we're grieving someone alive and well. Tati Mimose should not be the second gap.

I stop on the last step and suspiciously look behind her. "What did you do?"

"Who, me? I don't keep secrets," answers Mom, patting the pockets of her denim skirt. "At least not *on* me."

"It's only written all over your face," I tease.

The truth is, my mom is looking more like Grandma Rose these days. She has that same Deep Disappointment furrow in her eyebrows, except Mom's is more of a Deep Worry. Her usually high cheekbones seem flatter, and the bags under her eyes scream "sleepless nights."

Mom is my rock. She's right up there alongside my other rock stars, Grandma Rose and Tati Mimose. But Mom has got to find a way to forgive her sister. The problem is, Daddy and I are too afraid to tell her this. Whenever we do, she gets all in her feelings. Lately, Mom and emotions aren't a great mix. It's been hard enough watching her grieve her own mom.

I haven't told Mom that I'll be seeing Mimose today, which I'm feeling kind of guilty about. But I remind myself that it's better this way. My choices are to deal with the guilt of not telling her, or the guilt of telling her and watching her sulk over it. She's fretting about her big day as a vendor anyway and doesn't need the extra stress.

But maybe today, things will turn around.

It's just like that gospel song that brings my mom to tears when she listens to it on house-cleaning Saturday mornings.

Sometimes discouraged but not defeated . . . There're times I don't understand / But I believe it's turning around for me.

If I'm being completely honest with myself, I can admit that the Caribbean Christmas gift I desire the most is reconciling two of my favorite people on the planet. That I'd finally stop being their tug-of-war rope and be a bridge instead.

I accept Mom's hug and feel time suspend as I'm overcome with a sense of what her embrace is saying to me. *I know you're hurting. I'm hurting, too. But we can get through this. Together. Grandma Rose would want us to.*

We're both fighting back tears when we pull apart.

"What's going on?" I ask, my smile shaky.

"Come dance for your blessings," she answers.

"Happy birthday to ya, happy birthday to ya!" Daddy's singing voice warbles as he chaotically body-rolls over. He knows I can't not laugh when he looks like that. My dad has perfected the formula of making his dad jokes so boring, they're funny. It helps that he has this earnest-but-goofy smile. It kills every time he flashes it.

I follow Daddy's conga line, doing the two-step behind him, but stop in my tracks when I see my birthday setup.

The bay window blinds next to the dining room table are usually closed because our neighbor's house is so close to ours. But this morning, the blinds are open and sunbeams shine onto the giant rose-gold *1* and *5* balloons floating high over an arrangement of smaller multicolored balloons. Carnival feathers, beads, and sparkles are strewn around the breakfast spread on the table. All my favorites are here—scrambled eggs, breakfast potatoes, flaky croissants, lemon poppy seed muffins, and mountains of strawberries. I can't understand how my parents got all this done between the hours of two and six a.m.

"Is this where y'all ran off to when you stepped out late last night?"

"Never mind about that, just smile for the camera," my father says.

Even though I'm teary-eyed and in my *Avatar* pajama shorts set, I let my parents take pictures of me at the table.

"Come on, let me see that Destin smile," coaxes Daddy, who demonstrates by flashing the most staged grin on record. I laugh when I see it.

"Yeah, just like that," he says, completely misinterpreting my reaction.

"Just like what?" challenges Mom. "That's a Benoirs smile she has, thank the good Lord." She photobombs me, placing her cheek next to mine to compare smiles. "See?"

Daddy doesn't snap the shot.

"Take the picture," Mom says without lip movement, like a ventriloquist.

"Daddy, take it!" I shout playfully. "My cheeks are starting to—"

Snap.

My dad examines the mid-whine pic he's just captured of me. "Oh yeah, she's looking just like a Benoirs here."

It's nice seeing my parents this playful. They've been in financial crisis mode lately because of the restaurant. And I admit I've been spending way more time in my room than with them.

"Oh, so it's about clowning the birthday girl?" I ask in faux anger.

"Get him!" Mom barks.

Daddy's best defense is to pick up a bowl of strawberries and offer it to me with puppy dog eyes. We all howl with laughter.

This small family of three can get so loud. Funny how I never considered us a family of three. Though I'm an only child, with my grandma living here, and Mimose swinging by so often, we always felt more like a family of five.

After a few more pics and a pig-out session, our mini party is over as quickly as it started.

Mom gives me a mushy kiss on the cheek. "Now go get ready. Knowing you, you plan on ironing everything you'll wear—accessories, too!"

"But it's barely six thirty."

"Your mom's got this fear someone will take her corner spot if she doesn't get there at the crack of dawn," explains Daddy.

My plan is this: I'll go to the vendor site to help my parents set up. Then I'll tell them I have to run all the way back home to make sure that I unplugged my iron. Then I'll go meet my aunt, meet Renee, meet Papash (!), and return to the Port-au-Princesse booth in time to help my parents with the parade rush.

It's a good thing Renee and I ran through a quick dress rehearsal of this plan on Saturday. We timed it and everything. It should all go smoothly.

I hurry to my room to get dressed in my outfit for the parade. It turns out that my jeans don't work as well with the flashy off-the-shoulder top I bought with Renee. So I pair the top with denim shorts and it looks cuter.

My twists are unraveled, and I debate pulling my hair back in a ponytail. Sometimes boys at the parade like to ride up behind you and dance too close, so a ponytail positioned right at the back of the head can double as a prod to push them back and twist-slap them. But my shoulders look extra bare without my hair hanging down, so I leave my tresses loose.

It's only when my parents and I get to the coveted corner spot, all of us carrying aluminum pans of food, that I realize I'm still wearing my gold necklace. I've worn it almost every day since my grandmother gave it to me when I was nine. But wearing it to the parade? That's a rookie mistake. Carnival is too crowded and too touchy-feely to risk the chance of someone unclasping my necklace without my noticing. It would be a bold move, but odder things have happened.

I don't want to take the necklace off and put it in my pocket, either. The safest place for it now is around my neck.

I finish helping my parents set up right in time for my eight thirty a.m. meetup with Tati Mimose. My mom totally brought my plugged-in-iron excuse, and she rushed me off. Quicker than expected, I get to the Eastern Parkway address that my aunt texted me this morning.

I know this building. I've seen it on social media. Then I make the connection.

Kwame lives here. The same shiny yellow sports car from the pic he posted on Instagram is parked outside.

Kwame lives in the same building where my aunt is doing her reading?

I didn't expect Caribbean Christmas to be this magical.

Before I can text Renee this news bulletin, I see Tati Mimose walking toward me. My aunt is talking to someone who probably is a fan. They are likely asking her to interpret a dream. Or it could be another marriage proposal. Whatever it is, I'm sure Mimose has got the perfect the-answer-lies-within-you or develop-the-qualities-you're-attracted-to-in-me statement to throw the ball back in that person's court, before she sweetly sends them on their way. Right on cue, she waves when she sees me and ends her conversation with a gentle smile.

My aunt is looking hot in warm tones. She wears a ginger-colored tube top and paprika-colored leggings, like she's just stepped off an island spice rack. Her leggings are accented with waist beads and a slender brown leather waist purse. She's a Caribbean Cinderella, the belle of the ballers, and she's making a grand entrance.

"Happy birthday, Cissy-mama!" she calls to me. "Don't you look beautiful?"

"Thank you!" I say with an excited wiggle. "But look at you! Amazing as usual."

It's not just my aunt's style that makes her stand out. She's got a roller-skater stroll, as if she's gliding on mini wheels, strutting and flicking her wrist to a beat. Her whole choreography is a dance to the street rhythms. I can see it in the way she eyes the pavement like it's no different from her home's hardwood hall-ways. Indoors or out, I'm sure my aunt knows where her valuables are hidden or where her comfort food is stashed. She knows the secrets of these streets.

"Thank you, baby," Tati Mimose coos. She holds out her arms and I melt into her warm hug like I'm nine years old again. When she pulls back to study me as a fifteen-year-old, her smile erupts into a pout.

"You're wearing your necklace?" She eyes Grandma Rose's gold chain around my neck.

I grimace. "I know—I completely forgot to leave it at home . . ."

"Don't worry, I'll hold on to it in my pouch for you," she offers. Her waist purse looks like it's more fashion than function, but when she unzips it, I catch sight of her cell phone in there.

"Thanks!" I say, grateful to be with my quick-thinking aunt. I unclasp my necklace and hand it to her just as a bus barrels down the street, blasting us with turbulent air. My aunt goes all wobbly for a moment and I catch her elbow.

"Whew, that's one powerful necklace," Tati Mimose jokes, clutching the swaying gold chain as she tries to regain her footing.

I chuckle. "Well, that's because Grandma Rose was one powerful woman."

"Was?" My aunt looks at me sideways, and I feel one of her pronouncements coming on. She secures the necklace inside her pouch, then faces me. "She *is* powerful! What, you think that kind of power dies? It wasn't even born in her—it was passed down, which means it lives on in all of us."

I feel a little shiver down my back. I love when my aunt talks about the spiritual intelligence of women—particularly island women, and especially Haitian women. She could go on and on about the special brand of knowing embedded in our lineage. When I was younger, I liked to point at random countries on a map and ask, "What about folks from here?" and she'd retort, "They may come close, but we're even *more* powerful."

Now my aunt links her arm through mine and we walk up to the building. Kwame's building.

"Whoa," Mimose suddenly says, looking a bit dazed again. She stops and touches her hand to her forehead.

"Are you all right?" I ask. Did she skip breakfast? Like me, my aunt gets mad extra on an empty stomach.

She nods. "I'm fine. I'm just trying to remember if I have all the materials that I need for the reading." She begins ticking items off on her fingers. "I'll need Juste to provide the Florida Water, but I'm sure he has that. Most people want a reading this time of the year, because it's still like a beginning for them, even if they've been out of school for decades. It shouldn't take too long and then we'll be on our way," she adds, looking at me.

"No worries," I say. As excited as I am to go meet Papash, I'm in no rush to leave this building yet. I inspect the windows, half expecting to see Kwame looking out of, or sitting on, one of the ornate fire-engine-red fire escapes. These are the streets he walks on and the sights he sees every day. It's a little busier than my block, which is on a tree-lined side street off the main ave.

After a short wait to be buzzed in, we enter the lobby. The echoes off the marble tiles have a particular din. Once upon a time, when this building was mostly upper crust–occupied, the din may have sounded grandiose. But today there's a full and robust echo with a little bite to it, like a strong cup of Café Bustelo coffee.

But there's one sound—a familiar voice—that strikes up and down my spine like a xylophone. A calm murmur, followed by the low rumble of a chuckle.

I'm pretty sure that's Kwame's voice I'm hearing. Or is it just my imagination?

"Let's take the stairs. It's only three flights up," says Tati Mimose.

"Sure," I say.

Right when we climb up to the second floor, I'm at the point where my breathing is getting heavier. Just as I pant like a dog to make my aunt laugh, I see Kwame standing in the doorway of apartment 2J, talking to an older boy I recognize from school.

So it *was* Kwame. He's the voice! And he's here now, standing just a few yards away.

My xylophone spine is playing a jazz solo, and my heart is keeping time. When Kwame looks my way, he's clearly surprised to see me in his building. But he recovers quickly and gives me a nod and a slight smile. I try to nod in return but I'm not sure I manage it.

As my aunt and I head up the next flight of stairs, I hear Kwame's friend say something but I can't make out the words. Kwame answers in his trademark baritone: "Aw, naw, it's not like that."

Wait. Was that in reference to me? The friend continues to hype him up, but there's another chill "Naw" to smooth out any misunderstanding.

I rewind and play the subtle smile he flashed me. What is wrong with me? I'm going to meet *Papash* today, and I'm thinking of a boy from class?

As we reach the next landing, I take out my phone and text Renee.

At the reading with my aunt and Kwame is here!

Renee responds immediately. *He's AT the reading?*

No, I passed him in the hallway. He lives in this building.

What?!

I keep texting, half paying attention to what my awesome aunt is telling me.

"This won't be a ceremony or anything—just a quick tarot card reading. With the parade going on, everyone is on a happy high and the spirit world is here for the party. That's how I know it won't take long for spirit messages to come through."

I nod but continue to be distracted by my exchange with Renee.

He smiled at me and I froze like an idiot.

"But it's not like I'll become possessed or anything."

I blink and run Tati Mimose's words back. "Wait. What?"

She waves a stylishly long-nailed hand as we walk down the third-floor hallway. "Nothing, girlie. Forget I said it. Like, how often do people really have to break the glass and pull the subway emergency brake?"

I frown. "M-more often than you think?"

What does my aunt mean? Possessed? Suddenly, I remember the ceremony I witnessed when I was nine—that moment when my aunt was not herself. Is that what she's talking about now?

When we reach her client's apartment door, I hear drummers

playing inside. Cool. I imagine the scene waiting for us, and I'm eager to see the two or three drummers all sporting ceremonial white and playing the finest handmade tanbous.

My aunt pauses to touch her hand to her forehead again. She must be hot from the climb up the stairs. Then she regains her composure and pounds over the noise of the drummers inside.

"But what happens if you do get possessed?" I whisper, worried. "Didn't I just hear you say something about spirits crashing our big human party?"

My aunt's client answers the door before Tati Mimose can answer me.

He's wearing an oversized, color-block button-down and saggy jeans that make him look like a flashy, aging '90s hype man. His Colgate smile drops as soon as he sees me standing next to Tati Mimose. It's clear he expected her to come alone.

"Cicely, meet my client Juste," Tati Mimose says matter-of-factly. "Juste, this is Cicely, my niece and favorite plus-one," she adds, her tone affectionate the way it is when she brags about me. "She's riding along with me today. I hope you don't mind."

Juste's eyebrow quirks, and when he looks at me, there's an unmistakable clench in his jaw.

Oh, he minds. And I'm getting a strong sense that maybe we shouldn't be here.

CHAPTER FOUR

Our entry into Juste's apartment is a one-two punch. First, Tati Mimose stumbles the moment we step over the threshold.

"Whoa," she says.

Second, the front door thunderclaps shut behind us, which is mad startling.

I glance down at my aunt's ornate sandals, wondering why she tripped. Tati Mimose seems just as mystified. We flash each other grins at the randomness of it all and shrug before following Juste down his cluttered hallway.

We're forced to navigate an obstacle course of old vinyl records and stereo speakers of various sizes and from various eras. Juste stops to point out some albums to my aunt, who I can tell is impressed with his collection. Each time we stop, my eyes land on yet another strange decor choice. Like, what is a life-sized cutout of the actor Tom Cruise doing propped against the wall? The edges along its shoulders are a bit dented, which, I imagine, reflects how many times Juste has leaned his heavy arm there for a photo.

Everyone's got their heroes. I'm not going to judge.

Despite all the drumming, there's an eerie stillness to his home. At least I'll get to see live musicians in their element. I can't make out how many drummers must be in the living room up ahead. *Three, maybe four?*

We step into the living room, and an HGTV crew couldn't have pulled off a more surprising reveal. There are exactly zero drummers up in this piece. There is no band in the living room. Just speakers blaring drumming music. That's a letdown.

Juste has the room set up like a séance scene from the movie *Ghost*. There are candles everywhere and incense burning.

"Sit, sit, sit," he tells Mimose. "It's such an honor to have you here."

There's a round wooden table with two chairs. Juste brings over another chair, and I sit as close to possible to my aunt.

"Do you have a Florida Water?" Mimose asks Juste.

"Oui, I'll get that," he says dutifully. Somebody is clearly a huge Mimose fan.

When he comes back with the bottle of perfume, my aunt gestures for him to sit across from us. He complies and then barks, "Siri, play Vodou ceremony playlist."

Soulful vocals hold a lonely a cappella note before Haitian tanbou and conga drumbeats drop in and back up the singer.

Tati Mimose digs into her pouch, pulls out cards, and chuckles. "I won't need that for the tarot card reading."

"Siri, lower volume to two." Juste nods his head. "Cards? But I was hoping to speak to the lwa of lost love. Surely, you can do that for me."

In Creole, the word *lwa* literally translates to "law," from the French "la loi." But in Vodou, *lwa* means "spirit." Now and then my aunt posts a video explaining a certain lwa's personality and characteristics. And yup, like the traits of zodiac signs, they are all different. It's a lot to wrap my head around, so I can't say I've retained much info.

"Non, mon cher." Tati Mimose tries to sweeten her *no* to Juste. "That's not possible for me today."

Juste frowns. I pull out my phone and text Renee again.

Hopefully the reading will be over soon. But right now, this dude is giving me bad "Molly, you're in danger, girl" vibes.

Too bad it's too late to warn Tati Mimose. I glance at her to see that the incense, the music, the Club Spiritworld vibe suddenly have her in an altered state. She's seated before her cards, swaying to the sounds. It's like she's buzzed on the kind of spirits that come in a bottle. She stares at the candle flame before her.

"Is it hot in here? I could use some more air," she says.

My aunt definitely doesn't seem like herself, and this puts me more on edge.

I watch Juste get up and struggle with an ornery window. The moment he's got it open, a whoosh of warm summer air hits us. Yet I feel a chill.

"Thank you," says Tati Mimose. "Now let's settle in and relax so we can get started."

Juste sits back down, but he doesn't relax. Instead, he grabs a bottle of Haitian rum. I'd recognize that label anywhere. Almost every Haitian household has a spot reserved for Barbancourt rum. A world-famous brand with a badass, if-you-don't-know-you-betta-ask-somebody rep, one of the oldest family businesses in Haiti. Which means Juste is breaking out his good stuff for Tati Mimose's reading.

"Before we start," Juste announces, "I wish to bestow a shower of blessing to you for all the good work you do educating people about our sacred traditions."

Juste hangs his head back and takes a huge gulp from the bottle. But instead of swallowing it down, he *sprays* the rum from his mouth and showers it over Tati Mimose!

I'm stunned. Juste has a self-congratulatory look on his face, as if he's expecting his nonexistent drummers to applaud him.

"Why'd you do that?" I scold him. "Tati, are you okay with this? I know you wouldn't want your outfit stained."

My aunt seems totally chill. She's swaying slightly from side to side with her eyes closed.

I'm so caught off guard by her indifference. Something's not adding up. I've seen enough of my aunt's IG Live card readings to know that being human-sprinkler-system'ed is not part of the equation.

Unbothered by my outrage, Juste barks, "Siri, raise the volume to seven!"

I lean forward in an attempt to catch Juste's eye. "Bruh, my aunt clearly said she doesn't require ceremony music."

I might as well be the main character in a movie titled *People Juste Completely Ignores* because he doesn't comply with my request. Instead, he's marveling at my aunt. The way she's swaying, she's clearly under the influence . . . of something.

I flash back to the last time I saw my aunt behave this way, and I feel like that little girl staring from the living room shadows again. But this time, I speak up.

Panicking, I shout, "Siri, turn volume down to zero!"

Suddenly, my aunt's eyes open and she gasps like she's just surfaced from water. She surveys the room like she hasn't been in here before. I realize that her features have shifted, like she's trying on a new character.

Impersonation.

I shiver. Wait. No.

"Tati? Tati? Mimose!" I call out.

My aunt mumbles something unintelligible. The moment I wonder what it is she's saying, a tingly whoosh of air blows against my face, pricks my ears, and trickles along the back of my neck and down my spine. What is happening? This feeling takes me back to childhood, when I witnessed my aunt leading the ceremony. I felt the same sensation then. And it has the same effect today. Because, oddly, I can now understand the words my aunt has uttered. It feels similar to when someone is speaking Haitian Creole and my brain processes the translation in real time.

"What do you mean, Mimose has checked out?" I ask, incredulous.

Where is my aunt if she's here but not here? Who is this person speaking through her?

I remember what she told me in the stairwell. This can't be.

Is my aunt possessed?

Juste looks just as puzzled. But when he grasps the gravity of the situation, he turns to my aunt with renewed vigor. He shouts out a name that sounds something like "Erzu-lay!" and adds, "Is that really you?!"

I jump to my feet, ready to grab one of Juste's vinyls and hurl it at him like a Frisbee. "Erzu-who?" I cry.

Juste looks pleased with himself. "Wow. My first time spraying and I've called her here!"

Erzu-huh?

I remember that my aunt posted about Erzu-something-or-other once, in one of her the-more-you-know Instagram captions. I narrow my eyes and strain to recall morsels of info. All I can recall is something about the spirit Erzu representing femininity and beauty.

Which is all well and good. But if my aunt is this Erzu spirit right now, that means she can't exactly show up to meet Papash for the podcast. I don't care if I have to carry her; I have to get my aunt out of here and figure out what's going on!

My aunt speaks again, and again I understand what she says.

"You're not a queen, you're a squatter!" I shoot back at her.

This is outrageous. And it's all Juste's fault. That criminal.

"This is spiritual malpractice! Bring my aunt back, now!" I yell at him.

Juste ignores my pleas, possibly because his face seems frozen in a surprised state. His eyebrows can't get any higher and he looks at me like I'm a unicorn.

"You are a translator!" he cries. "Of course, I should have known."

My face must be translating that I'm confused because Juste explains. "Has no one taught you? Some spirits or lwa speak in a sacred language and need manbos to serve as interpreters."

"What's a *manbo*?"

"Someone like you, a Vodou priestess."

My eyes pop out in shock and my breathing quickens. I'm not a Vodou priestess. I'm a fifteen-year-old girl from Brooklyn!

A fifteen-year-old girl from Brooklyn who clearly can translate what a mumbling Mimose is saying as the spirit Erzu.

Juste's intensity is starting to creep me out. He takes Mimose's—or is it Erzu's?—hand. "Now we can communicate. Please, I need answers!"

This guy needs to slow his roll.

"Uh," I improvise, wondering what I can say to get rid of him so my aunt and I can slip out. I need to get her home. Maybe a cold shower will snap her out of this. "Earlier, she said something about needing five minutes alone to meditate."

"Of course," says Juste, eager to be accommodating.

"Alone," I repeat.

"Yes." He jumps out of his seat. "I'll just, uh, use the bathroom."

"She says make it ten minutes," I interrupt in faux channeling mode, ignoring my aunt's real request that Juste and I compliment her beauty. This Erzu is one vain spirit.

"Let's go, whoever you are," I whisper to my aunt as soon as Juste has slammed his bathroom door shut. Using my fear as a muscle, I hoist her to her feet.

But the spirit who is piloting Tati Mimose's body closes her eyes, shakes her head, and digs in her heels.

"We gotta go—now!" I snarl through my teeth. If my heart pumps any louder, Juste will think Siri's put on the drumming playlist again. "What's it gotta take for you to move? This is serious!"

Tati Mimose/Erzu begins communicating her demands. Her long, graceful fingers graze her neck and cup both her wrists. Her meaning comes across clearly to me, the way my childhood invisible-ink kit would slowly reveal messages, one word at a time.

"You can't go out in public looking and feeling this way?"

I whisper as I steal frantic glances in the direction of Juste's bathroom. "Lipstick? And perfume?"

Thinking fast, I grab a tube of lip gloss from Tati Mimose's waist pouch and slather it on her pouty lips. Next, I grab the bottle of Florida Water and Erzu instantly bares her neck in my direction. I spritz along her collarbone and let the sweet scent perfume the air. Erzu looks like she's been doused with a luxury brand. She's giving me runway-model face, but that's short- lived. She raises a wrist and shakes it. She's demanding more.

"More jewelry?" I ask.

She grunts her assent.

I take off my five-dollar macramé Haiti bracelet that I bought off a vendor and put it on her wrist. Erzu keeps her eyes on the bracelet as she twists her wrist this way and that.

"Now let's go."

But it's too late. Juste's toilet flush announces his impending exit. The bathroom door creaks open. Ew, he's nasty—he didn't even wash his hands. I close my eyes in defeat, wondering how I'll manage to extract us from this place now.

The shrill of a ringing cell phone pierces the air. Juste's phone.

"Ma commère," Juste booms into the phone. His bathroom door shuts again, muffling the rest of his conversation.

Whew!

"An ale," I say. "Allons-y. Vámonos. Let's bounce. Whatever the heck language you understand." I tug Tati Mimose by the forearm with hopeful energy. Finally, she follows me and we practically parkour our way down Juste's cluttered hallway, past the vinyl records and Tom Cruise. I open the door as quietly as possible, and we head for the staircase.

But in this spiritually buzzed state, Tati Mimose is treating the stairs like escalators. She stands elegantly in place as if she's gliding down mechanized stairs at some upscale department store.

At this rate, we'll never make it out of the building.

A thunderclap slam breaks out, and I'm just as unprepared for it as I was the first time. Especially because now this means Juste has left his apartment.

"Mimose!" Juste bellows with palpable rage. "Come back right now! I prepaid for this reading!"

I feel Juste's anger hit me like hurricane-force winds. It has always been said that people's energy enters a space before they do. And Juste's energy is pretty mucky.

My heart bounces but I hold still. I hear Juste's feet stomp down the hall, and I realize he's heading for the elevator and hasn't seen us. Now I'm grateful for Tati Mimose's frozen pose. There's one bead of stress sweat streaming from my forehead and I'm afraid if it gets to the bottom of my face, it will drop to the stairs with a loud *plop*. But the hum of the elevator doors opening confirms that Juste is bypassing the stairs. I'm relieved that he's clearly not about that daily-step-count life.

As soon as I'm certain the elevator doors are shut, I hook an arm around Tati Mimose and practically drag her down the next flight of stairs. I know Juste will be outside the building waiting for us. And I don't think he's about to be friendly. At all.

We're on the second floor. Kwame's floor. I glance at 2J. Someone has just walked into the apartment, and the door is gently closing as I hear Kwame greet the person. There's laughter and palm-slapping. I do the quickest thing I can do in this situation. I let go of Tati Mimose's arm and race over to grab the door before it shuts.

CHAPTER FIVE

"Kwame? Kwame?" I call, trying to whisper. I lean close to the doorframe and peer through the open sliver.

Those ink-black eyes I remember from school appear.

Kwame.

I ignore the electricity that xylophones down my spine again. Now is not the time.

"Can my aunt and I come in?" I whisper. "It's kind of an emergency."

Kwame looks out into the hall behind me and asks, "Aunt?"

I turn around in a panic and see that Tati Mimose is standing a few feet away, staring, mesmerized, at the way light bounces off her bracelet. She's out of Kwame's field of view. I hear Juste getting off the elevator down in the lobby, still shouting angrily for Mimose.

Before I can second-guess myself, I grab Tati Mimose, open

Kwame's door all the way, and step inside his apartment, closing the door softly behind us.

Kwame's apartment smells like popcorn. It's also nice and cool, and I instantly feel my stress sweat drying. The loud, persistent hum of an air conditioner window unit almost drowns out the excited voices of guys gathered in the living room. They are hyped up like they're debating the top five lyricists in hip-hop or playing a heated game of spades.

We're standing in an alcove that's fitted with a floor-to-ceiling bookcase. It's an impressive sight. The books are mostly historical texts, the neatly lined-up spines showing a range in subjects from the Mali Empire to Mansa Musa's riches and Queen Nzinga. The cozy chair and footrest in the corner look like an invitation to curl up with one of the books and travel back to precolonial times. If I were visiting under different circumstances, I'd do just that.

"Nice to meet you, Cicely's aunt. I'm—"

Tati Mimose couldn't ignore Kwame more if he was a fake gold chain. She floats over to the bookcase and runs her languid fingers along the books' spines like they're piano keys begging to be played.

Kwame raises a questioning eyebrow at her before looking to me.

"Come on in and make yourselves at home," he mumbles, not without a bit of irony.

I shrug one shoulder like, *You know aunties.* But the truth is,

I have no plan. I figure I'll just try and hide out here until we lose Juste. Hopefully my aunt's client thinks we've gone to the parade and he won't come back to the building for a while.

"What's got you so shook?" Kwame asks me. "You said there was an emergency?"

I appreciate the sincere concern etched into the lines across his normally smooth forehead. And I also appreciate the protective flash in his dark eyes.

But his opening the door again and poking his head out to eagle-eye the halls is something I could do without.

"Would you stop?" I whisper-scream behind him. "Come back in!"

"What? Who's after you?"

I suck my teeth. "Come back in and I'll tell you."

He does and leans against the door to face me. There's a mischievous twinkle in his eyes.

Whatever. I look cute. And it's my birthday. I'm not going to shy away from that stare just because I need his help. That's nothing to be ashamed of. Everyone has mayhem when they least expect it.

I anchor my feet and stare back at Kwame with fifteen-years-of-age energy. "Your parents home?" I ask.

Kwame shakes his head. "You know you don't have to make up excuses to come to this party." He smirks. "How'd you hear about it anyway?"

I sigh dramatically, with a glance at Tati Mi—ugh, who am I

kidding? That woman reading a book upside down is a whole Erzu.

"It's not an excuse. It's legit."

Kwame looks at Erzu before whispering to me. "Did you get in trouble at school again? Does your aunt know?"

I pout. "What do you mean *again*? I'm never in trouble."

He grins. "Well, then how come we're always meeting like this?"

I cross my arms and give him a look.

"Don't worry, I would never think of crashing a party with your friends," I snap.

"Actually, it's more like my older brother's friends."

"Why didn't you invite *your* friends? What, you don't want your boys seeing your collection of action figure miniatures?"

"Who told you about that?"

I laugh, loving the release of tension from my shoulders. "Lucky guess."

I look to my left and find a gaping absence in the spot where Erzu was feeling up the bookcase. Then a cheer breaks out from the living room. When Kwame and I peek in there, we both gasp. Erzu is holding a bottle in the air as she maneuvers through the small crowd of older high school kids like a flight attendant with a drinks cart.

"Oh, damn. She must've found my parents' stash."

I bolt over to my aunt, Kwame following close behind me.

"Whoa, whoa, whoa, it's not that type of party," Kwame

says, carefully removing the glass bottle from Erzu's hands.

"Relax, bro, she's just messing with us," says a tall boy from our school. I remember that he was honored last year for being among the students who scored the highest on AP exams in Kings County. During a school assembly, he talked about how he and his two brothers had been homeschooled, and they were only entering high school and middle school in these last two years. He admitted he was worried he'd be awkward socially, but he's found his tribe.

Now that I find myself studying his profile next to Kwame's, I see the family resemblance. Shiny dark eyebrows, angled cheekbones, the same unwavering stance.

"*She's* messing with *y'all*? You sure it's not the other way around?" Kwame challenges him.

"You need to save that energy for them corner boys you hang with," says AP Boy, unruffled.

Kwame looks cut down but not enough to retreat. He huffs, "Right, 'cause anyone who's ever checked you for good reason is a corner boy."

Erzu is now giggling and wagging her finger. There's no way she can meet, much less interview, Papash in this state. The only desperate choice is to wait it out here until Tati Mimose hops back into the pilot seat.

But how long will that take? I've got about an hour, two max, before my parents start looking for me. And I'm supposed to be working the booth when the parade starts.

I can't just do nothing.

I fire off a quick SOS to my bestie.

My aunt's client was on some Vodou vengeance and now my aunt is literally not herself. Need reinforcements!

Renee responds right away.

Dissatisfied customer? But how could he tell her predictions are wrong if they haven't happened yet?

It's not like that. And she's not a fortune teller. Anyway, she's possessed!

As in . . . ?

As in some spirit has hijacked her body and we need to lure my aunt back.

As in you're really being serious right now?

Yes. Our-Papash-meetup-is-in-jeopardy serious.

Say less. Send me the addy. I'll grab a few things and be omw.

For a second, I forget that I'm in a room full of people until Kwame pulls me back to the scene in progress. "Yo, Cicely, meet my brother Sekou."

I look up from my phone to see AP Boy studying me out the corner of his eye. I can't tell if he's trying hard not to smile or if his mouth is just fixed that way.

"Oh, I see you skipped inviting your friends over and went straight to inviting your girl over," says Sekou.

"Real Gs move in silence," quips a boy wearing a Brooklyn Nets jersey.

Sekou nods. "And that 'aunt' is the perfect 'chaperone.'"

The way my body's embarrassment trigger is set up, my whole face gets hot. It feels like the sun just walked into the room on two legs. I'm suddenly mad at the air conditioner for being loud and wrong.

"Cicely, you don't have to listen to this. We can go talk in my room," says Kwame, not realizing until too late he's said the exact incorrect thing in front of this crew.

"Baaa!" erupts the room.

Erzu shimmies to the chorus of teasing that breaks out. My grip around her shoulders is about as tight as my smile right now. There will be no shimmying on my watch.

Kwame sighs and walks away, motioning for me to come with.

My arm still around my aunt, I follow Kwame down the hall to his bedroom.

"Sorry about my brother," he says. "He's an idiot."

I'm still processing everything that's happened. And yes, my excuse for coming to Kwame's place couldn't look and sound any more stereotypically Haitian if I tried. What's more embarrassing: a bunch of kids teasing Kwame about possibly dating me, or my aunt being possessed and everyone finding out about it? What if they recognize Tati Mimose as the Vodouista influencer and Erzu loves the attention she's getting? It's bad enough she immediately found the parental stash. Thank goodness no one pulled out their phone to record that one.

"You can sit anywhere you like," Kwame says, shutting the bedroom door behind us.

Tati Mimose free-falls backward onto the full-sized bed like it's a pile of snow.

"I'm, uh—" I turn to Kwame, but he holds up his hands.

"How about we take a short break from apologizing on behalf of weird relatives. Cool?"

I sit down beside my aunt with an exasperated sigh. "Cool."

It feels relaxing to sit, but not enough to fall asleep, like my aunt clearly has. I gawk at her peaceful face, even though I'm grateful she's switched off for the moment.

"So what happened?" Kwame asks, leaning back against a waist-high wooden dresser.

I ease the tight grip I've got on my embarrassment and tell him what went down upstairs—the reading, Juste, and the possession. Thankfully, Kwame doesn't throw holy water on me. He keeps a neutral look on his face, like he's auditioning to play an extra in a movie.

"What can I do?" he asks.

It's just the right question, but I don't even know where to start. I glance at Mimose.

My aunt is still powered off, looking like she's floating on her back in still waters. I've seen the actual Tati Mimose do this mermaid act in swimming pools before. She likes the idea that being a Pisces means she's at peak performance when water touches her skin.

I process that thought for a split second before turning to Kwame. "Do you have a cold washcloth?"

I can't exactly put my aunt under a streaming shower in his house, but maybe this will be the next best thing to get Erzu out. Besides, a cold washcloth is the answer to almost anything that ails the head—migraine, headache, fever. I'm not sure if it's her brain that's affected, but I need to try and wake my aunt from this state. And how long will that take? My stomach twists. Forget my own selfish desire to meet Papash. If Mimose doesn't show up for the podcast, that could be disastrous for her career.

No. Her skipping out on Papash is not an option. Everybody knows Mimose to be a show-up-show-out professional—point, blank, period.

"I'll be right back," Kwame tells me.

When Kwame leaves the room, I'm free to openly stare at my surroundings. His room looks like it's been decorated by an adult. I imagine his mom or somebody selecting and installing the sensible slate-gray bedsheets and matching, weighty window curtains. But it's obvious Kwame added all the room's accents himself—from the Michael Jordan silhouette decal and framed graffiti art on his walls to all the Afrofuturism novels and the collection of Wakanda's Dora Milaje warrior figures—in miniature—on his shelves. (Lucky guess, for-real-for-real).

Impatient for him to get back, I stand up and walk over to examine his vintage Octavia Butler books.

"Look who stopped by," Kwame says when he returns.

"Renee!" I shout with relief. My bestie looks super cute in her ruffly red, black, and white top and frayed denim shorts. I'm especially happy to see the bulky tote she's carrying on her shoulder. "I'm so glad you're here."

She takes one look at a zonked-out Tati Mimose and rushes over to give me a sympathetic hug. "I'm so sorry you're dealing with this, today of all days."

"This is a no-apologies zone for the moment," I whimper into her shoulder.

"Well, I'm not gonna let this ruin your birthday," she says when I pull away.

"You brought supplies?"

"Everything I could think of." She nods, holding the bag open to me.

My face falls when I look through her tote and find . . . a makeup bag and a clip-on LED ring light?

"What? Mimose is always down to post a fresh video," Renee explains. "You know she can perform her way out of anything."

"Huh?" I shake my head. "You can't perform your way out of a possession. This spirit has set up shop and doesn't seem to be budging."

If Renee had an idea light bulb floating over her head, it would be short-circuiting right now. She takes a studied look at my aunt sleeping on Kwame's bed.

"Oh," she says quietly. "When you said 'spirit' I assumed you meant, like, the spirit of self-doubt. Interviewing Papash is a huge deal, so who could blame her for making up an excuse not to do it?"

The spirit of self-doubt. That sounds like something Renee's pastor would say. When I'm bored of my mom's church, I go with Renee to her more youthful church services. The music is so much better there, and so are the motivational sermons. Her pastor is always trying to cast out spirits of a different kinds—like the spirit of laziness that's keeping kids from working harder, or the spirit of lack that sucks money from adults' pockets. It's amazing thinking of life's obstacles as actual sabotaging forces trying to keep humanity down to add more hopelessness in the world. I would pay to watch that Marvel movie.

But this isn't that scenario.

"She's not pretending to be possessed to get out of the interview," I tell Renee. "The woman is possessed by a Vodou spirit called Erzu-summin'-like-that."

"Sis, c'mon," Renee says, twisting her bunched-up lips.

"I wish I was playing, but I saw it with my own eyes."

Renee wordlessly puts a hand to her bare collarbone, where her crucifixion pendant is usually hanging. Unlike me, she remembered not to wear her favorite necklace to the parade today.

I turn and reach for the washcloth Kwame is holding out. My exchange with Renee has made me aware of the dull pang of shame digging into my side.

"How do you reverse this?" Kwame asks with a chin point to my slumbering aunt.

"Is this dipped in holy water?" I ask, but my joke doesn't land. When my eyes meet his, I drop the act. "I don't know . . . I don't know anything," I say. If I sound embarrassed, that's because I am.

Tati Mimose gives a slight smile when I place the washcloth on her forehead. She seems soothed by it. But she squints when a bright light suddenly shines on her face. I turn to its source to find Renee holding the plugged-in ring light in the air, angling it this way and that.

"I don't think that will help," I say.

"So what will?" Renee asks.

I shrug, feeling despondent.

Kwame coughs out his words with a rasp of mockery. "Your aunt is like this popular priestess and you're clueless about voodoo?"

Is dude laughing at me?

"Well, one thing I do know is it's Vodou, not *voo-doo*," I snap. I'm close to shouting and I can't help it. I'm riled up. "I saw one ceremony when I was little, but no, I never took a class on all the ins and outs of it. My parents' whole hustle is throwing shade at Mimose because she dabbles in Vodou and they don't approve. Hard to believe, but not everybody's got an African name and African history books filling their shelves like you do," I tell him defensively.

Kwame shakes his head. "That's my parents, not me. Their thing has always been that our history didn't start with slavery, and that we should know about who we were and what we had going on long before Africa was even colonized. But in none of

79

those lessons did they ever get into spiritual practices and belief systems."

Renee lowers the ring light and says, "I don't know everything about my Trinidadian and Tobagan culture. And J'Ouvert is a Trini creation."

I appreciate what she's trying to do to make me feel better about my lack of knowledge. But for some reason, it does little to shake off the chip that Kwame's question dropped on my shoulder.

"And hey," Renee continues. "We're not even a hundred percent sure what we're dealing with here, so there may not even be a need for a Vodou expert."

I open my mouth to protest because *really, Renee?*

She holds up her hands in surrender. "And maybe that's my ignorance showing, but the point is, we each have a lot to learn."

Kwame lets his body fall back against the wall and crosses his arms in thought. I suddenly feel the tension I've shoveled into this room, and my irritation shifts from Kwame to Renee to myself.

Shoulders hunched, heads hanging, the three of us inwardly sulk over our shortcomings. We're floating like astronauts in zero gravity, except there's no enjoyment in it. Being cut off from a big part of ourselves and our heritage feels like being untethered and set adrift. The most we can do is try and grab at anything anchored, even if it's not familiar to us.

Suddenly, a young boy pops out from behind a window

curtain, and Renee and I both scream. He's holding a tablet, and he looks sort of like a miniature Kwame.

Actual-sized Kwame is scowling at his mini me like he just stepped on Kwame's bright white Jordans.

"Yo, if you don't get your scrawny—"

"Before you wild out, I can help," says the quick-talking boy, pointing to his tablet screen. I can just make out the partial headline on the web page. One word stands out: *Possession*.

"You're the one who needs help, out here creeping on grown folks' conversations. Get out!" Kwame reaches for the tablet, but the fleet-footed kid ducks away just in time.

"Wait a minute," I say, totally taken in by what's on the boy's screen. "Let's hear what he has to say."

Renee nods. "It's not like we were getting anywhere."

"Yeah, Kwame," says the boy with a puffed-up chest. "What they said."

"Everybody," Kwame says through clenched teeth. The boy, who seems about eleven or twelve, ducks from Kwame's grasp again. "This is my sneaky baby brother, Kofi. Y'all I'm sorry—"

Sneaky is putting it mildly. But I don't have a leg to stand on. I glance at Mimose/Erzu. *My* relative isn't even standing.

"Uh-uh-uh," I say in all sincerity. "Apology break, remember?"

Kwame nods and breathes out a soft chuckle. I smile at him, sensing a tingly feeling traveling up my arms.

"So, you guys are a bunch of know-nothings." Kofi's

announcement is as abrupt as the ads that cut into my YouTube viewing. "Well, that's what Google's for. I searched 'home remedies for reversing a Vodou possession' and found a list of items."

"How about a home remedy for a forehead knot removal?" Kwame warns, but Kofi ignores his irate brother and waits for a reaction from me.

I'm skeptical.

"How do you know that list is not from some whacked-out conspiracy site?" I ask. "I just know haters are putting all kinds of lies about Vodou online, working hard to keep folks thinking it's some devil-worshipping cult."

"Exactly," says Kwame.

Renee walks over to examine Kofi's screen, which she compares to something she's pulled up on her phone.

"This blogger," Renee says, nodding at Kofi's screen, "is someone your aunt follows on Insta. It must be legit."

I shake my head in disbelief, and then I nod the go-ahead. "Let's hear what it says, then."

Kofi's slender face lights up and he begins reading. "It says we need some rum—"

"Rum?" I interrupt. "That's what the dude at the reading mouth-sprayed at my aunt."

"Eww," Renee squeals in an octave deeper than her speaking voice.

I slow blink at her. "I'm thinking that must've been the moment he put that possession on her."

"So, you're saying you'll actually go along with this random list?" asks Kwame with a wince.

I shrug. "I mean, what other choice do we have at this point?"

Renee looks down at her black-and-red sneakers.

"Okay, rum. I can check my parents' stash," offers Kwame. Before he leaves the room, he draws in a quick breath as if he's about to advise us against actually following this list. But then he thinks the better of it and walks out.

"Keep reading," Renee tells Kofi, wholly curious now. I guess she's wondering how far we're willing to take this. "What else do we need?"

Kofi continues, "Florida Water, prayer beads, a fetish— whatever that is—"

Renee's eyes go wide. "Is it fetish in the way I'm thinking?"

I don't think so, I mouth to her to protect Kofi's ears from grown folk talk. I'm pretty sure I've heard my aunt mention the word *fetish* on her socials in a spiritual sense, but I can't remember what it means.

I search my phone and find it. "Fetish," I read aloud. "An object that is thought to contain magical powers."

"Oh, whew," says Renee.

"What else is on that list?" I ask, twirling my hand at Kofi to keep us on track.

"A medicinal plant, whatever that is. A mojo bone—"

"Say what now?" I ask, creeped out.

"I wish I was kidding," laughs Kofi. "I'm pretty sure they

mean an animal bone, though, not a graveyard bone, like in the hoodoo tradition."

Renee and I look at each other like we want to pretend we didn't hear any of this. If our memories wipe clean the last two seconds, maybe it would mean we don't have to act on that . . . item.

"Shall I go on?" Kofi asks, his eager eyes darting from my face to Renee's and back again.

Kwame walks into the room then, heaving out a sigh that's not quite loud enough to wake the still-slumbering Tati Mimose. We all look at him expectantly. "My parents have every type of drink, except rum," he finally explains.

"This really ain't a Caribbean household," Renee mutters.

Kwame goes back to lean against his dresser. He glares at Kofi. "What are you waiting for, someone to beg you? Keep going."

Encouraged by his brother's interest masked as exasperation, Kofi reads on. "And y'all need something called a hex pouch, and finally . . . a high priestess to perform the ceremony."

"Is that all?" I ask.

Kofi doesn't get that my question was rhetorical. "Well, I can also tell y'all what you'd need if this were a Catholic exorcism, or if you were chasing away a Hindi or Jewish spirit. The list is mad similar . . ."

"How do you even know that?" Renee asks.

Kofi's shiny eyebrows rise. "I always over-research a subject for my clients. You never know when a trick question will pop up."

"Still writing essays for them bullies, huh," Kwame says, before turning to us with his thumb pointing at Kofi. "My brother makes business plans for his forced labor."

"There's no wrong way to launch a start-up," Kofi retorts.

Renee and I are poorly hiding our amusement at the Hilliard brothers' exchange.

Kwame walks over and punk-snatches Kofi's tablet.

"Hey!" Kofi complains.

"I want to see this list for myself," Kwame says.

"Mind if I check it out first?" I ask. Suddenly the list feels personal to me. I guess because it is.

Kwame hands the tablet to me, and I turn my back to him as I read it. I feel the warmth of his presence as he reads over my shoulder, and try to ignore the static charge prickling my cheeks. As a distraction, I clear my throat and read the list out loud:

1. *Rum*
2. *Florida Water*
3. *Prayer beads*
4. *A medicinal plant*
5. *A fetish*
6. *A mojo bone*
7. *A hex pouch*
8. *A high priestess*

"That's not overwhelming at all," Renee deadpans.

Kwame reaches his arm around and points to item number seven. "I think I know what a hex pouch is. In fact . . ." He shuffles over to his top desk drawer and rummages through it until he finds and holds up a tiny burlap bag, the size of one of his Wakanda figurines. "I have one," he says. I listen for notes of irony in his voice, but there's none to detect.

"You just happen to have that lying around?" I ask, half joking.

Kwame smiles at the pouch he's now turning over in his hands. "My nana in Alabama got it for me the last time I stayed with her. The summer I was obsessed with that book *Hoodoo*?"

It takes me and Renee a second to realize he's asking us if we've read the book. We're both suddenly leery of giving him the wrong answer.

Kwame rapid-blinks his lush lashes at us. "The thriller? By Ron L. Smith?"

"Maybe if I saw the cover?" I offer as a way of letting him down gently.

It takes no time for Kwame to grab the book from the short stack on his bedside table. He keeps it too close to his pillow *not* to still be obsessed with it. The book has so many dog-eared pages, I wouldn't be surprised if it started barking.

"Yo." Renee takes a step closer, clearly fascinated.

And thankfully, I recognize the cover illustration of the glowy-eyed black crow, wings outstretched in a mid-swoop attack, its open beak no doubt squawking its only warning before those claws land on an unsuspecting person's head. I'd love to read it someday.

Kwame takes in the look of recognition on my face and nods his satisfaction. "I thought my nana would be scandalized when she saw the book title, but she asked me if I had any questions. I hit her with so many, she took me to this traveling museum that was all about Southern Hoodoo. We got this from the gift shop," he adds, holding up the hex pouch. "It's supposed to be for protection."

"A protection charm," I say, amazed. I bashfully thank him when he hands it to me.

"Quiet as it's kept, Southern folks got their traditions, too," says Kwame.

"And quiet as it's kept, he still won't let me borrow his precious book," Kofi butts in.

"Get your own." Kwame's eyes are playful, even as he barks at this brother through gritted teeth,

Renee sees me eyeing her tote bag. Without a word, she holds it out to me and I place the hex pouch in there for safekeeping.

"Yay, we got one item!" Renee cheers.

Kofi gives her a high five. "Seven more to go," he says. "A lot of these things, you're not gonna find at the corner store."

I think of what I saw in Juste's apartment. "The man who caused this had Florida Water," I say. "But there's no *way* I'm going back to his place."

"Prayer beads are easy enough to get," says Renee, reading

over my shoulder now. "My granny's got a few in every room in our house."

I nod. My mom owns a couple of rosaries, plus she inherited all of my grandma's. Where does one even get rosary beads from anyway? They all seem to have materialized from the ether. I would probably believe the person who tells me rosary beads grow on trees.

I focus back on the list. "But where do we even start to look for a mojo bone?"

Kwame runs a hand over his face. "This is some next-level alternate reality here."

"I know." I gesture to the sleeping Erzu. "But I'll do whatever it takes. My aunt can't stay like this. And she damn sure can't interview Papash in this state. I know how important today is for her—"

"And for us!" Renee adds. "No cap, we were all set to meet Papash today."

"It could still happen!" I say, even as the thought of my child-hood curse creeps into my mind to tell me that things this amazing don't happen to me.

"We need to focus on the list, remember?" Kofi points out.

"We could get everything on this list, but it won't mean a thing without a high priestess, right?" says Kwame.

I nod. "Then I say we start there. Let's find someone who can help us first."

This will be tough to accomplish, because everyone who is

anyone is either across town at J'Ouvert, or busy prepping for the parade.

A carnival drumbeat ringtone goes off. Tati Mimose, clearly still Erzu, sits up, lazy-eyed and giddy. She slowly bounces her shoulders to the beat and sways her head from side to side.

"Someone's calling her," says Renee.

I walk over to the bed. "Let me answer that for you, okay?" I say to Erzu, pointing to the pouch around her waist. "I'm gonna reach for the phone in your purse."

Erzu's head falls back when she looks at me, and I think of the time my mom said Tati Mimose's head was swollen by all the attention she gets. Is Tati Mimose's dome too heavy a load for this spirit?

I recognize the name on the screen. It's my aunt's intern, Jovita.

"Hi, Jovita . . . intern," I answer painfully before I can stop myself. It's the only way I could think to clue in everyone about who is calling.

"Happy Papash Day," Jovita responds, in a tone a lot flatter than you'd expect from that type of greeting. "Just confirming that you're on schedule, and reminding you that I'm good to meet for a beauty refresh if you need one before the interview."

Renee, Kwame, and Kofi start pointing at the phone and making wild gestures like this is family game night, so I put the call on speaker. "Uh, this is her niece, Cicely. Mimose is—er, unavailable right now, but I'll pass on the message."

Erzu stands up and does a twirl.

"Great," Jovita says. "I'll keep my phone close in case she needs me."

Renee, Kofi, and Kwame start waving their arms and pointing again, and I nod, because I've come to the same conclusion: Jovita might be able to help us locate a priestess.

"B-before you go," I say. "I was just having a debate with my friends, and I was wondering—is there any priestess who can, say, remove a squatter spirit out of a person?"

"Squatter?" Jovita echoes.

I look at Erzu, who is now nosing around Kwame's room. She's currently drawn in by his mini action figures.

"Yeah, like, say a person is possessed, just for example. Who can get the spirit to, uh, vacate?"

"A good high priestess can do that."

"Yes, but let's say we'd want to find one, like, now? Just to maybe interview them about this, uh, debate we're having . . . for school," I improvise.

"Um, what about your aunt?" Jovita suggests.

"Well, she's busy right now, so do you know of anyone else? Uh, hypothetically. Someone my aunt would approve of, maybe?"

"There's Nuna," Jovita replies. "She's actually at J'Ouvert at this minute, doing the spiritual blessings for a pan band."

I bounce on my toes and pump my fist. "Can you text me the location where she'll be, and we'll head over?"

"Yeah. I was just texting with her—uh, but not because I'm doing any side intern work for her or anything," Jovita explains with a forced laugh.

"No, of course not."

"Great. I'll text you when I hear back from her."

I hang up, smiling.

"My aunt's intern says there's a priestess blessing the pan band at J'Ouvert!" I report. "She's still there, but we gotta hurry."

"Guess we'll have to go to the danger zone that is J'Ouvert," says Kwame, and my heart squeezes, because it's not lost on me that he said *we*. The feeling ends abruptly when Kofi splashes a cold dose of reality in my face.

"If you ask me, everything I read on J'Ouvert sounds like a ghoulish nightmare. Pretty eerie stuff, and that's not even if you factor in all the shootings that keep happening there."

"What other choice do I have?" I say, uncertain. I check the time. "It's nine now and there's about three hours till the podcast taping and less than two hours till the parade starts."

Kwame and Renee agree, yet no one moves a muscle.

"I appreciate all you've done for me today, truly," I say, looking from Kwame to Renee. "But I wouldn't blame you for sitting this one out. Especially you, Renee. I know your great-granny wouldn't want you anywhere near J'Ouvert."

"Neither would your parents," Renee says. "And there's no way I'm gonna leave you to deal with this alone."

"Same goes for me," says Kwame.

My eyes meet the defiance in his for a split second, because I'm too smitten to hold his gaze a moment longer. "Thank you," I sigh.

"What are y'all waiting for? Get going!" shouts Kofi, with the boldness of someone who isn't coming along. "I'll stay here and you can check in with me if you need anything."

That's not a bad idea. Renee clearly feels the same way because she's already giving our cell numbers to Kofi.

Kwame and I get to work, luring Tati Mimose away from his Wakanda collection while Renee pokes her head into the hall to see if the coast is clear. Tati Mimose squeezes Kofi's cheek, and then hooks an arm around his. I take her other arm.

"Now!" whispers Renee, leading the way.

Kwame and I peek around my aunt and nod at each other before tiptoeing across the hall to the front door, successfully avoiding Kwame's older brother and the pregaming crowd.

Somehow I doubt the rest of this mission will be as smooth sailing.

CHAPTER SIX

It's been a minute since I've been in a dollar van.

When Grandma Rose and I would venture far from a subway stop to visit her homies—her nickname for her former high school students—we would catch these uniquely New York commuter vans. Today, Renee, Kwame, and I decide that taking one to J'Ouvert will be easier than trying to navigate the subway with Erzu.

We stand on the corner of Franklin and watch a dollar van pull up. The doors open and it's a rolling United Nations of the Caribbean in there. The many versions of Caribbean Creole meet Spanish-speaking delegates all under one roof. The speaker of the house? The radio that's currently blasting chest-pounding reggae riddims.

It comes as somewhat of a shock to me that today of all days, there are passengers wearing hard hats, hairnets, health-worker scrubs, janitorial uniforms, and restaurant-kitchen whites. These are the people who do not have a momentous day like today off, and it humbles me to realize how naive and privileged I could be in thinking all of Flatbush is exempt from obligation on Labor Day.

"All right, Rasta."

People thank the driver as they step off. They're older passengers in crisp shorts sets, classic Panama shirts, and plastic sun visors, all looking ready to claim a good parade-watching spot.

"You riding?" the driver calls out to me, Kwame, Renee, and Mimose.

Mimose/Erzu waves flirtatiously at him and smiles. I tighten my grip on her elbow.

I can sense Kwame's and Renee's hesitation as they take in the crowded van. Some people—even city kids—don't like to be in close quarters with strangers. But I actually don't mind. If there's a narrow spot between two people on the subway, I'm not above claiming it. Especially during winter when I'm trying to stay warm.

I grew up with an appreciation for this type of incidental closeness. I'm talking the basic human closeness of the non-creepy kind. I've had my hair braided, countless times. I've sat under straphanging passengers on buses and trains. To me, it's an experience akin to sitting under the bower of a tree. You're basically sitting under the bower of a human. And on some molecular level, it feels like I'm in nonverbal communication with that human; that closeness offers me a particular sense of their personhood I wouldn't get in other exchanges.

I wonder if this type of closeness keeps my sixth sense functioning. Or if it works some awareness muscle most people don't often get to use. And when that muscle works, it's a kind of magic.

Kwame hops into the dollar van first and scoots down the seat to the window. I follow, handing the driver eight bucks to cover all of us (technically, the dollar van is the "two-dollar van."). I get sandwiched in between Kwame and Tati Mimose, leaving Renee to the other window.

Although being in close quarters with strangers is a nonissue for me, I am not so sure I'm ready for this type of closeness with Kwame.

I never imagined I'd be trying so hard to avoid his eyes' gaze and his skin's graze. Our shoulders are flush against each other, and it takes 'nuff mental mojo to tune into the lively conversations popping off in the rear row. The topic of discussion is "favorite steel pan band." The way folks are shouting from deep in their chests, you'd think they were arguing—when in fact, they're in emphatic agreement.

"Number one band for the last decade is Nerves of Steel," hollers a gruff voice.

"Case closed. Discussion over. Plate clean!" shouts another.

A third voice chimes in, "Nerves of Steel ate everyone and licked the plate."

"No crumbs left. Every year them smash it," replies the gruff voice.

The whole exchange makes me chuckle, yet it's still hard to relax, given the current state of things with my aunt. As the van gets moving, Mimose/Erzu closes her eyes and seat-dances to the reggae riddims. She may be otherworldly, but when the beat drops, her movements are still bound by the laws of physics—she sets off a human domino effect when she hip-bumps me, and I shoulder-bump Kwame.

Tuh!

I shoot Erzu eye daggers, and she returns a self-congratulatory smile that makes me wonder whether she did that by design.

"S-sorry," I offer Kwame out the side of my mouth.

He answers with this odd, angled half nod.

Being this close to Kwame Hilliard is making me act more awkward than usual. Maybe it's the same for him? Like a book, I want to take cover.

Renee has retreated to her phone—everything around her melts away when that girl gets to reading headlines—and Erzu is still dancing to the rootsy sounds of the driver's playlist. Today of all days, it's hard to hate on anyone who has such a deep appreciation for island music.

The seats vibrate as the beats travel through the van. The driver stays alert, his head on a swivel as he looks out for passengers and, possibly, also the police.

"Bless up, Rasta," a young woman hopping off the van calls to him at the next stop, as more passengers make their way on.

I wonder what Tati Mimose—the real Tati Mimose—is

thinking right now. And *where* is she right now? Is she somewhere observing helplessly from afar? Is she overwhelmed with panic or floating off in ignorant bliss? Where did she vacate to, if at all? It's hard not to overthink this.

I'm also trying not to overthink why Kwame is now putting his window down like he desperately needs air. He's probably wondering what he's gotten himself into. I surely would be wondering that if a boy from school I barely knew knocked on my door asking for help with a possessed uncle. Like, who does that?

Yours truly, that's who.

There are double doors on Kwame's side of the van. At the next yellow light, maybe he'll do the stuntman roll right out into the street. The embarrassment of this whole day threatens to swallow me whole just as Kwame turns away from the window to say something. I take a breath and wait for him to rightfully peace out of this madness.

"Happy birthday, Cicely," he says.

I hope it's not apparent that my cheeks are burning. "How did you—"

A sheepish look crosses his pretty face, and his eyebrows form an upside-down V. "Back there in my room. I heard your friend mention it."

"Oh," I breathe. "Thank you."

Kwame gestures to something in his hand. "This is all I could think to give you last minute."

I'd been so submerged in the depths of his eyes, the miniature

Shuri figure in his hand went completely unnoticed. When I finally see it, I can barely locate my voice.

"Aw, I can't take that from your collection," I manage to say.

"It's okay. I had two," he assures me. "This one's yours. It could be like a good luck charm. Since you're like Shuri—you know, on a mission to help someone you love."

I must be a Disney character, because I hear harps when he says the word *love*.

Get it together, Cicely!

Our hands meet as I reach for Shuri, although our fingers don't touch.

"Thank you."

We hit a pothole, and Kwame and I bump shoulders. No apologies are exchanged this time. I thumb the contours of miniature Shuri's signature coif.

Then I turn around to check on how my best friend is coping with having Erzu for a seatmate.

"You okay?" I shout to Renee over the music and the lively discussion still going on behind us in the van.

Renee doesn't hear my thin voice at first, because she's showing cat videos on her phone to Erzu, who is mesmerized by them. Erzu jumps in her seat, startled by something that's cracking Renee up.

"See? They almost always land on their feet," Renee tells her.

I'm not sure if Erzu is catching the meaning of Renee's words, but the shea-buttery-smooth tone of Renee's voice subdues her nonetheless. That girl's voice has got range.

When Renee catches my eye, she answers with a thumbs-up.

Thank you, I mouth to her. Renee chuckles at my grateful grimace.

My best friend is thriving despite this bizarre new dilemma on our hands, and it sets me at ease for the first time this morning. As utterly bizarre as this situation is, it's clear Renee and even Kwame aren't here to shame me. Whew.

I reach over to hand Renee my Shuri gift. "Can you hold this in your bag for me?"

"Is this an item from the list?" She looks hopeful.

"No, it's, uh—it's mine."

"Where'd you get this? It looks like the pieces I saw in Kwame's room," she says with a glint in her eyes.

Erzu claps her hands at the surprise ending of another cat video, motioning to Renee to play another one, and her timing could not have been better for me.

"At least somebody's happy," Kwame shouts over to us.

"No human or spirit is immune to a good cat video." I laugh, more out of relief that it seems Kwame didn't hear my exchange with Renee. I look over at the video playing now.

"Where do you think people go, in times like these?" Kwame asks, echoing the question I was thinking just moments ago.

"I'm not sure," I answer, turning my attention back to him.

He rubs the side of his chin in thought. "I've never even passed out before, or been under anesthesia."

"I didn't think of it like that," I say, sitting with that thought. "But same. I've never experienced anything close to it, either."

"As many times as I've been bonked in the head with a basketball, I don't know how it feels to slip from this consciousness."

"You can probably thank your tall 'fro for that," I tease.

Kwame looks squarely at me now, his eyes smiling. "I use to wear my hair tall *freshman* year. You noticed me from back then?"

My cheeks burn once again, but I play it off with an easy shrug. "I—I may have hid behind it in the cafeteria line once or twice. You know how intense that one dude behind the counter gets."

Kwame smirks and studies me for a second. "Right."

I force myself to focus on the steel band discussion behind us, which is intensifying. Instead of wondering, *Did Kwame notice me last year, too?* I'm all, *Who knew there was a fantasy pan band draft and a fantasy league?*

"What about you?" Kwame asks.

"No, my hair wasn't much different last year," I answer without thinking.

"What, you bringing the headbands back?"

I touch the top of my head where the groove that announced my headband habit used to be. He noticed?

The lip curl at the corner of Kwame's mouth says of course he noticed. It's also saying he's one-upped me because *he* was bold enough to make it known that I was on his radar last year. And he knows that he was on mine, too. I smile and shake my head.

"Uh-huh," he says with that knowing gleam in his eye. "Play it how you wanna play it, though."

I drop my head and smile. But remembering the story behind those headbands makes me go still and quiet.

After Grandma Rose died, I had zero energy to fuss with my hair, so headbands were my solution. For, like, months.

Maybe Kwame catches me drifting to a sad place, because he picks up our earlier conversation.

"I've watched TV shows like *Supernatural*, where a spirit takes over a body," he says with a glance at Erzu.

I blink. "Yeah, and it's always like the person is caged somewhere, banging on their gate, crying to come out." I shake my head and swipe two fingers across my forehead.

I hope my aunt is all right. When she returns to her body, will she wake from it all like it was a dream? Will she have any recollection?

Kwame leans back in his seat. "Yo, what if it's like wearing virtual headsets and she's still able to experience everything going on, only from a safe distance?"

"Maybe," I say.

Or maybe it's like daydreaming about your first kiss. Your eyes can be trained on what's in front of you—the streets out the dollar-van window—while you're seeing a vision playing out in your mind—Kwame leaning in close, our foreheads gently meeting before our lips touch—

My phone buzzes with a text. I jump, then pull it from my pocket.

It's a message from my mom, no doubt wondering where I am. *How you making out?*

Thrown by her phrasing, my phone almost pops out of my hand. *What does she mean?! I'm not making out with Kwame!*

Kwame looks over, confused by all my fidgeting. Why do I have my phone up so bright? I try to hide Mom's text on my screen, angling my phone away from him as I thumb my response.

All good. Iron unplugged, whew! Ran into Renee, though. Be back in about an hour.

I hope she knows I'm speaking in CST. In Caribbean Standard Time, one hour translates to about two hours. I of course leave out the tiny detail that I'm currently driving *away* from the parade route. Toward J'Ouvert, where I'm not allowed to go. And that I'm with my aunt, who is currently possessed.

When I shift to return my phone to my back pocket, my leg brushes Kwame's. The "making out" question pops back in my head and I'm jarred all over again.

I make an effort to look everywhere but in Kwame's direction. The skinny bottle of cola champagne in the driver's center console captures way more of my focus than it should. I study it like it's enshrined at the Louvre.

In trying to make out the flavor of the liquid sloshing around in it, I notice the label is missing. It's not clear if the bottle used to carry Ting, Cola Lacaye, or Solo Kola in its former life. It's amber in tone, like a lot of Caribbean sodas, but thanks to all the sloshing it's doing, the drink is flat, not fizzy.

The driver rolls down his window as he races through a yellow light, and another eerie whoosh jerks my head back. Something's up with that bottle.

I lean forward and whisper-scream to Renee, "I think that drink is on our Erzu Rid List!"

"Cola Couronne's not on the list," answers Renee, but I ignore her because I need to speak up while I have the gumption to.

"Drinking and driving?" I shout over the reggae beats, cautiously teasing our driver.

"Eh?" He swivels his head in my direction.

"She's asking if that's alcohol in that bottle," Renee booms in that amazing way she can.

"You talking 'bout this rum?" He lifts the bottle I've been eyeing.

"Rum?" Kwame shouts.

I scooch to the edge of my seat. *It is rum!* Okay. The hex pouch and rum make two items on our list. We've got this. We can still turn this baby around, rid Tati Mimose of Erzu, and meet Papash with nary a hair out of place.

"Rum is made from sugarcane, the island crop our ancestors cultivated during punishing centuries of slavery. It connects us to the islands, to that history," the driver says.

"Can we have it?" I blurt out. Loud and clear this time.

The driver glares at me in his rearview mirror. "You expect me to give a bunch of underage kids hard liquor? This is not no party bus."

I wince through a smile. "What if I tell you we need it for spiritual purposes?"

He hangs his head to the side and lets out an open-mouthed laugh. "In my hands, this rum here is first and foremost used for spiritual reasons. Proper. Because I bless the van daily."

Erzu seems pleased by this news, because she keeps nodding and reaching forward to give the driver an approving pat on the shoulder. I grab her hand and hold it so she doesn't get us kicked off.

"How do you do that?" I ask, genuinely curious.

"Sometimes I splash a bit on the hood, other times I spray the spirit from my mouth."

Renee, Kwame, and I all gape at one another. It's clear we want to start drilling the driver for answers, but we keep cool heads as I continue my line of questioning.

"But why spray it from your mouth?"

He shrugs mid-maneuver around a double-parked car. "I let the spirit guide me, and I do what's on my heart."

"Spraying is the ancestors' way," speaks up the woman sitting beside the driver in the front passenger seat.

The woman sitting right behind me sniffs. "Back home, we call that demonic."

I turn around to catch a frown pulling down her face. She seems like the type who is only happy when she's not happy.

"What's demonic about performing a blessing?" snaps another passenger.

"Keep fooling yourself," answers the frowning woman. "Pretend you can't understand why the island with the most suffering and natural disasters is the main one practicing Vodou rituals God don't like."

"Whoa," says Kwame, twisting to glance behind us. "Say you're anti-Haitian without saying you're anti-Haitian."

I sense the dread creep in. Prejudice from your own people is like a lethal brand of betrayal. And I hate how ostracized it makes me feel.

I've heard the whispers before—about Haiti being in some Bermuda Triangle of trauma, churning with natural disasters, political instability, poverty, and other iterations of bad luck and wrongdoing. Whispers that Haiti can't catch a break because the nation and its people are cursed. Whispers that everything from earthquakes to corrupt leaders are just punishments. They trace the curse back to an unapologetically Vodou-flavored pre-battle prayer ceremony held centuries ago, which led to the Haitian Revolution.

Then there are those who don't whisper this theory, but shout it. Much like the delightful passenger behind me, they pump anti-Haitianness into the air and then have the nerve to advise you to take a deep breath. Well, not today.

"Renee, remember in eighth grade when Ms. Simmons showed us pictures from her Ghana trip?" I ask loud enough for the hater to hear. "I wonder if God *likes* that colonizers built their church on top of slave dungeons so they can check in on their human property after Sunday service. But never mind that—let's dump on the remixed rituals that carried people through."

Even as I confidently say it, a small part of me is worried that defending Vodou's spiritual rituals is some kind of Class A heavenly felony that carries a purgatory afterlife sentence. That must be my mom's influence rubbing off on me. I look to Renee for reassurance. But my bestie is uncharacteristically quiet. She's taken a sudden interest in the scene out her window.

I've never, ever been ashamed of my aunt for a second, and I'm not about to start now. I protectively loop my arm through hers and steel myself for the hater passenger's slander. All she does in response is suck her teeth and grumble. Erzu lays a head on my shoulder and coos into it.

"Do you call my rum ritual strange?" the driver pipes up. "You don't think it's strange when rich people-dem break a champagne bottle over a new yacht-so. Why can't I carry this in my minivan as a way to bless it? I shuttle around the community's parents, children, workers, caretakers. People who like to cook for people, care for people, nourish them. I want to keep them safe when there's trouble. I have a family who needs me, and I want to keep myself safe in these streets, too."

"Ya, man," says the woman in the passenger seat.

"I want to help the people-dem. I know a lot about these streets—more than those born and raised here," he boasts. "It's my job to go about things, and to know where a person can find a such-and-such, whatever that such-and-such means for that particular person."

Tati Mimose's phone buzzes then. When Erzu places her hand on my aunt's stylish pouch, I gesture my apologies to her before reaching in and taking her phone. I feel a little like Sister Lucille doing it, but it's for the best. When I check the screen, I'm glad to see it's a text from Jovita. She hasn't forgotten about us. Best intern ever.

The priestess just left J'Ouvert to get herself ready for the parade.

What? My whole aura deflates. I feel like asking Rasta to turn this van around.

Maybe I shouldn't have smacked my forehead so dramatically, because Kwame and Renee are now peering over to read the text.

"You gotta be kidding me," says Renee. "So, we're heading out there for no reason?"

I hang my head, hoping to rattle the thoughts in there and see what falls into the ideas slot. But I got nothing, except for a few haunting words like *demonic* or *suffering* and a couple of *God don't like*s.

The phone buzzes again with another message from Jovita.

"Huh?" I say, reading it. "Apparently, the priestess is wearing this elaborate butterfly costume for her chiropractor office float."

"I wonder if she's an actual chiropractor," Renee wonders aloud. "Wouldn't that be wild?"

"Maybe we find something else from the list at J'Ouvert," Kwame answers in a sweet attempt at encouragement.

I suddenly remember what the driver said, about being able to help people find things. I lean forward again to speak to him.

"Excuse me," I say. "Would you know anywhere we can find a spiritual fetish?"

"What you need with that?"

"It's the hardest item to locate from this list," answers Renee. "That and the plant shrub thingy."

"Your party list?" the driver asks.

I shake my head. "It's a spiritual list. We promise you."

At the next red light, when Rasta asks to see this list, I show him the screenshot on my phone.

The yellowing whites of his eyes give a seat-dancing Erzu a quick once-over in the rearview mirror. "Thought she was filled with the type of spirit that comes in a bottle, but this makes more sense," he says.

"We were on our way to J'Ouvert to meet up with a priestess," I tell the back of his ropey locs. I feel like Oz-seeking Dorothy saying it. But it's all good because she's a girl who loved her auntie, too. "But we just found out she's already left from there."

Rasta raises an ashy finger. "Funny enough, I do know of someone who can help you get that fetish. And he's at J'Ouvert now. My old coworker Scotty is a school bus driver who is dropping off and picking up steel pan band members there today. Bus number forty-two, near the Grand Army Plaza arch—you can't miss it."

I feel a wave of relief. "Ohmygosh, thank you," I say. "That sounds great."

"But I must tell you . . . Scotty's a White dude."

Everyone in the van gasps.

"He moved to the gentrified area of Crown Heights."

More bellyaching and facepalms.

"You mean to tell me Carnival and J'Ouvert are getting gentrified now, too?" a passenger calls from the back.

"But hear me out, my bredren—for a White boy, Scottish Scotty is deep into dis kind of ting," the driver explains. "Gentrifiers may fall in love with a location or with the potential of a neighborhood, sure, but I'm talking about a love for the people. I know. I can tell you. Scotty is not here because he has nowhere else to be, or because it's trendy. He stays here out of love for the people. He was here before the bulk of the people coming and he'll be here after they leave again. Don't watch them. You know who the real ones are. I wouldn't send you to anybody who's not worth the time."

Unconventional, but I'll allow it. Though I've only just met this Rasta dude, I kinda trust his judgment. I'm sure for years he's been following the migration patterns of White folks who move to the ultra hip areas of Brooklyn in droves. With a keen eye, he's watched them inch closer and closer to farther-flung neighborhoods like our Little Caribbean. He can probably point out the real ones from the ones who hope all their neighbors clear out.

He continues. "There are things that people don't speak on that Scotty won't mind speaking to you about. I admit, there's an ability for the White people-dem to discuss taboo things we would be labeled anti-Christ for. Like goat yoga. A big part of Scotty talking to you openly about these things is because of that privilege. Fair enough. But he knows his stuff. He has an understanding that others are afraid to admit to. You can't miss his flaming-red hair. In fact, if we 'urry, we can catch him."

"Step on it!" his copilot passenger yelps, getting into our scavenger hunt, and I can't help but laugh at her outburst.

Kwame leans in and says to me and Renee, "It's all good now. If we can find this Scotty, it won't be a wasted trip."

He gives me a reassuring nod, and I try to reach for his optimism since mine has cut off so quickly. I hope he's right.

And then everyone in the van holds on tight as the driver floors it. The artist blaring from the speakers goes into a speedy, tongue-twisty reggae chat that matches our J'Ouvert-bound frenzy.

CHAPTER SEVEN

We pull up to Grand Army Plaza, the site of J'Ouvert. Looking out the van's tinted windows, I hardly recognize the familiar plaza. Today's scene is *extra* extraterrestrial. Every being in sight is chillingly otherworldly: all horned figures and painted bodies.

Kwame swings open the van door with deliberate bravado. He's about to plant his Nike whites on the pavement like Neil Armstrong when the driver gestures to the mob of grown people in their ghoulish costumes.

Rasta warns, "Watch out for the jab jabs. They like to prey on your fears."

None of us make a move to exit.

Jab jabs. The ghoulish J'Ouvert revelers Kofi chillingly warned us about. With reason. If the carnival is Caribbean Christmas, J'Ouvert is hella Halloween.

Throngs of jab jabs are out there, waiting for us to come out the van. You'd think they'd be tired by now. J'Ouvert starts the night before, and this is the closing hour. But nope. They're swarming, and they have their sights on us. Some of them are wearing horns on their heads that would frighten a peel off an orange. I see slithering snakes worn as necklaces and creepy pendants swinging from chains. Someone is wearing an unnerving set of googly eyeballs on his chest.

"Son, we haven't got all day," the driver tells Kwame. "I need to get going."

Kwame finally slinks out, and Renee and I reluctantly follow, our arms linked with Erzu's. Before he speeds off, the driver rolls down his window and pours out some of his rum before handing me the near-empty bottle.

He eyes me sternly. "This is enough to do the blessing, but not enough to drink."

I happy-gasp as I accept the bottle. This is amazing. I barely know what to say besides "Thank you."

"Bless up, sistren," he calls out before peeling off.

I turn around to hand Renee the bottle of rum, which she stashes in her tote bag. Erzu and Kwame are standing still, taking in the scene. Now more of the revelers have noticed us, the new arrivals. They start to crowd around as they dance and howl. I shiver. I know we need to move fast and find Scotty, but our path is blocked.

One dancer comes up screaming like a banshee and sneers in my face. My mind reaches for safe harbor and I think of the van driver's comparison of venerated versus vilified rituals. I tell myself these people could just as well be shouting from the bleachers of a football stadium. The painted chests. The mascot hats. The shouting. It all looks familiar and would be acceptable in a different context.

Some people get to express themselves at every game outing. Others have to wait for a time like this to let their demons out to play. This idea calms down my heart rate, and my breathing slows.

For barely a moment.

A person dressed like a goblin comes up and taunts me right in my face with bulging eyes and a flash of teeth. I notice their canines looking sharper than they should be, like a set of wolf teeth in a cavernous human mouth.

Please tell me those are fake? They gotta be.

Being here, in the midst of J'Ouvert, I am instantly confronted with the fears I've locked away. Namely, that this feels like a haunting, yet I half expect to hear bullets ring. I don't know which of these skin folk are my kinfolk. I don't know who wants to do us harm.

One jab jab flings a ton of thick powder up into the air. The fog of white haze sits and waits for a summer breeze that's not coming to clear it from view.

The whiteness before me suddenly becomes insistent, and bulging in appearance. Until I realize I'm looking at a pair of eyes attached to a menacing figure painted all in white. Two shadowy horns top its head. The figure approaches me like I'm prey. A prickly fear travels up my arms and curls its fingers around my throat.

I can make out the whole painted-white face now, its hanging tongue and grimacing expression. Every fear I've ever felt comes to the front of my mind.

And what I see most clearly now is the corpse of my grandmother. I vividly recall the moment I stood at the casket too long and stared too closely and could make out the thread sewn between her lips. I watched her eyes and wondered if they'd fly open. I'd wondered about the darkness underneath the ground, where they planted her. These same thoughts haunted me for nights after the funeral, and they're fresh now. Freshly summoned and being served like a plated dish to this goblin. The more I fear, the more he feasts. His maniacal grin is satiated by my terror.

I close my eyes and picture my grandmother lying in the coffin again. But now her face looks nothing like her own. She looks like . . . Sister Lucille! Her eyes fling open and she belches out one word: "Cursed." Her voice sounds like it's coming from the seat behind me, but then I remember I'm not in the dollar van anymore.

The vision pins me to my spot. This very spot, near corners that have seen the deaths of strangers. Blood has spilled on these streets in J'Ouvert celebrations past. Someone just like me, coming here for one purpose or another, had been pierced with a bullet that ended their life. Could it have been a moment like this, when they were pinned in place by fear? Or were they caught by complete surprise, partying one minute and lying on concrete the next? Does their soul now mingle with the other souls walking free in the streets today?

Renee touches my elbow, and I jump.

"We're going this way, Cicely," she says, and her bold voice is a relief. "Come on, let's get moving."

I can't seem to shake my fears, but I obey Renee. She leads the way with Erzu and Kwame beside her.

But the painted-white goblin follows, having latched on to something in me and liking what he sees. He jumps in front of me for a second time, arms in the air, crouched to my level so that we are eye to eye. He starts shaking his head and swaying, his mouth snarling all the while.

And it's not just one goblin. A wall of them have moved to block our path.

"Oh no," croaks Kwame.

It's a feeding frenzy, and they're not backing away.

I fear for our own lives now. How will this confrontation end? Are we in danger of cutting our lives short today? Have I put my friends and my aunt in danger? I shouldn't have brought them here. We are way out of our depth. Kwame looks like he might pass out, and I am helpless to do anything about it.

Could my aunt be recognizable to any of these people? If so, do they mean to cause her any harm? Is that why she's staring so hard at them right now? I don't blame her. All we see are bulging eyes shining and taunting us, like haunted house employees at an amusement park. Well, they're very good at their job, because we're very scared.

Another jab jab appears and barks at us, and Kwame screams.

I didn't expect that—the bark or the scream—and we all flinch and back away more. In doing so, Renee, Kwame, and I get crowded in and then somehow separated from each other. Someone grabs my wrist and when I look up, I see it's Juste. The angry client who was intent on finding my aunt.

I can't believe it. Did he follow us here? I'm too scared to even scream, but I struggle. I try to get my arm free, but his grip is too strong. When I look up again, though, my arm is free and Juste is gone. Is he here? Was he ever? Am I seeing things?

I manage to make my way back to Renee and Kwame. At this point, I want to turn around and chase down the van. But Rasta has gone, and with good reason.

What type of hellhole have I gotten my friends into? "You guys, I should have never brought you here," I say shakily. "I'm so sorry. Let's just go."

"We're not going anywhere," someone declares.

It's Erzu.

She is steps ahead of us. She puffs out her chest and points her chin up, making herself look so much taller than her five and a half feet. She waves her arms, as if directing traffic.

This motion distracts the jab jabs from their menacing as

116

they seem to size up my aunt. She doesn't yield. She stares right back at them, so fiercely that the goblin that had been boring its eyes into me blinks and looks away. And even more stunningly, backs away.

The fear suffocating my throat seems to ease a bit, its fingers loosening. My breathing is less shallow. The air is not as thick as it was a second ago. I feel protected.

And suddenly the taunting goblins and demons all move aside. They seem taken aback even as they obey.

Relieved, Renee, Kwame, and I look at one another like we just woke from a nightmare. We follow Erzu as we pass through the jab jabs' breached wall.

"Let's stay close," says Kwame, and he holds out his hand, which I accept, because we've just had a shock. But as our hands connect, I can't help but notice that his feels warm and caring. He's got that same look of concern on his face as he did when I knocked on his door in a panic.

Grateful, I glance up ahead at Erzu leading the way. There's something familiar about Erzu, I realize—her gait, her confidence. And something else. I can't place my finger on it, but deep down I'm sure I know this person. Could it be my aunt has returned? Warmth fills my chest.

I rush up to her, my fingers pulsing with excitement when I touch her shoulder. "You're back!"

But the same sleepy, drowsy eyes that meet mine are nowhere close to my aunt's usual fiery expression.

So, it wasn't that the jab jabs recognized my aunt. It was Erzu flaunting her power. Erzu is not just a jewelry-and-perfume-loving party spirit. She's also a fearless badass and wants everyone to know it. And for the first time, I'm accepting that she's here. At least for now.

"That was wild, but we got lucky," breathes Renee.

"Seriously," I say, relaxing a bit as we walk down the plaza. I'm now even able to enjoy the sounds of the Haitian bamboo trumpets and metal horns around us.

Kwame meets my gaze with this concentrated but oh-so-heart-throbbing focus.

"First time here?" he asks me.

I smirk but don't look away. He's clearly only looking at me and making small talk to avoid the sight of three jab jabs who are passing by.

He smirks back and I want to dreamy-sigh. "You don't miss a thing," he says.

"Have *you* ever been to J'Ouvert before?" I ask Kwame. "Renee and I have not."

"Only once," he says. "I came with my parents last year, because my cousins flew in from Alabama and wanted to check it out."

"I just read a piece about how tons of tourists are flying in for J'Ouvert and the parade," Renee pipes up. "The numbers are up there with the St. Patrick's Day, Chinese New Year, Pride, and Puerto Rican Day parades."

"All those other parades are in Manhattan, so that's a good look for Brooklyn," Kwame points out.

"But respect to Harlem," adds Renee. "That's where the carnival first got started."

"It did?" The parade has always been a fixture in my life. My family has been going for as long as I can remember. Yet I never stopped to think much about how the parade originally got organized.

Renee nods. "The whole thing was indoors in the winter, which is the same time that Carnival happens everywhere else in the world."

Right. Mardi Gras in New Orleans. Carnival in Trinidad and Tobago or Brazil. Those events all kick off the Christian Lent season—the perfect time to let loose before the season of restraint. "Oh, it must have been freezing to hold a parade at that time of year," I say.

"Yeah, that's why they changed it," Renee says.

Kwame nods. "My grandmother remembers. She used to go to the Harlem winter carnival back then."

"I always thought it was a Brooklyn thing," I say.

Renee smiles. "Of course you did. You barely ever leave Brooklyn, Cicely. Except to visit your cousins in Jersey."

I'm about to respond when our foursome gets split up again—Kwame and me on one side of a mob, Renee and Erzu on the other. This time, though, it's not jab jabs swarming between us but a cluster of kids sporting matching indigo shirts. Steel pan drummers without their steel pans.

My best friend's voice can be heard through the crowd. "They've probably just finished performing," Renee says to Erzu before the two of them rejoin me and Kwame. Whew.

The band is all girls, which is mad cool. It's a busy weekend for pan bands, because Panorama, the annual pre–Labor Day steel pan competition, took place on Saturday. I read the back of one of the drummers' shirt: WE REMEMBER THE FEMALE STEEL PAN PLAYERS OF THE 1970S AND 1980S. WE ARE THEIR LEGACY. When that drummer turns and looks our way, I give her a nod of deep respect.

The thin, bearded older man walking with the steel pan drummers looks vaguely familiar to me.

"Li'l Jessica's daugh-tah!" he calls out to someone in the distance. "Li'l Jessica's daugh-tah."

Renee reaches over Erzu and clutches my wrist. "Oh no! Could it be?"

She looks even more afraid than she did of the jab jabs. I hold her hand, and we both turn our heads and slowly glance back without detection, before whipping around.

Yes, it's him—Uncle Rufus, from our shopping trip! He's wearing that same BOTANY BAE T-shirt.

We cringe when he half turns and angles his face in our direction.

Memory of the man's dire warning not to go to J'Ouvert buzzes in my ear, and I wonder if it's a sign something bad will happen. Adults love the opportunity to say *I told you so*, and who knows, maybe he manifested that opportunity.

"Let's go the other way so he won't see me," Renee says, her face ashen. I know I'm not supposed to be at J'Ouvert, but the kind of trouble I'd get into with my guilt-tripping parents is nothing next to the agony Renee's great-granny will unleash on my best friend. That woman would probably get the church pastor and his first lady involved with doling out punishing lectures to poor Renee.

"What's going on?" asks Kwame.

"Come on, follow us," I say to him, and take Erzu by the hand. "We can't let that old man see Renee or word will get back to her grandma that she was here."

"Chloe's daugh-tah, yuh no hear me call you?" Uncle Rufus can be heard, scolding another person entirely. *Doesn't he know any boys he can call out?*

If Renee gets busted, it'll be all my fault. I'd throw a bag over her face if it would help hide her.

We rush through the steel band crowd until we come to a wall of writhing bodies dipped in black paint or slathered in white. Some of them are wearing horns; others are in frightening masks. Oh no. Not again. But these jab jabs don't seem to notice us; they are all entranced by their own dancing, embracing the darker depths of their souls.

Still, Renee, Kwame, Erzu, and I move as one unit, arm in arm.

Renee glances all around us. "I don't think we should linger. We need to get out of here as fast as possible."

I nod, pointing to a few yellow buses parked ahead, by the

Grand Army Plaza arch. That must be the drop-off for some of the bands. "We need to find the Scottish guy. He's got to be over there."

The people gathered by the buses look way less intimidating, even though their faces, sweaty and dusted with powder, bear the mark of J'Ouvert. They're mostly musicians with steel drums hooked around their necks.

But we have to walk through a few more painted goblins and demons to get there. My heart races and we all clump as close to Erzu as possible. Of course, Erzu can't resist being in the center with the revelers as they body-roll down the street.

"Erzu!" I shout, zigzagging around a few feral pirates, one of whom won't stop blowing her whistle so close to everyone's eardrums.

"I got her!" Renee shouts over her shoulder to me. She's close enough to grab Erzu's hand, which she does. But Erzu only pulls her deeper into the melee. I get logjammed behind the pirates. I turn around to find a detour and bump into a jab jab in scary clown makeup dressed in *Hamilton*-style colonial garb, down to the powdered wig and three-cornered hat.

I nearly swallow my tongue.

Kwame steps between us, even though I'm pretty sure he's terrified out of his mind. He reaches a shaky hand back, and I meet it with my own. Our fingers interlace, and our arms entwine as we steel ourselves, taking small steps back.

The clown makeup, the haunting getup, the maniacal laugh—
it's all close to sending me crying home to my momma. I can't deal
with another scary jab jab.

But then the small furry pendant dangling from Colonial
Clown's chain gives me pause.

"We run left on three," Kwame alerts me out the side of his
mouth. "One, two—"

"Wait." I squeeze Kwame's hand once. "I need to ask the jab
jab a question."

"You what?"

Unable to actually speak to the jab jab, I raise my shaky hand
and point to the furry pendant weighing down his leather
necklace.

Colonial Clown drops the menacing act to answer me. "What,
this? Rabbit's foot for luck," he says in a bouncy game show–host
voice.

"A r-real one, bone included?" I manage to peep out my question, still shook.

Kwame squeezes my hand once, silently acknowledging
what I'm getting at. Item number six on the Erzu Rid List. We
need that mojo bone. Still, poor little bunny.

"I never thought of it that way, but yes, with bone intact."

"Can I . . . have it?" I wince as I ask it, before trying to fix it.
"I mean, I'll buy it from you? If we can agree on a price?"

The smeared-smile makeup that before made him frightening now makes him seem cheerful. "It's not for sale, but I'm

happy to lend it to you. Just bring it back to the school in a couple of days. My classroom is still next to the music room."

"Mr. Harris, is that you?" Kwame shouts.

I rub my eyes and try to find the face behind the clown makeup. Is that really our US History teacher from Christian Prep?

Colonial Clown laughs his maniacal laugh again, only now I recognize that it rings more goofy than spooky. "A deadly jab jab was coming for you, and boy, did I cut him off just in time. I figured my kinda scare was more your tolerance level."

Kwame shakes his head. "Thanks, Mr. Harris."

"Glad to see you're not here with those knucklehead friends of yours," he tells Kwame. "Stay safe."

I gratefully accept the rabbit's foot, and Kwame and I beat feet to Renee and Erzu, who are just a few yards away.

"We can cross mojo bone off the list," I say, holding up the rabbit's foot charm with my free hand. But instead of checking it out, Renee smiles and glances at my other hand—the one still holding Kwame's.

"That's . . . lucky," she teases.

I let go of Kwame's hand, and thankfully, Renee lets go of the hand-holding subject. She takes the rabbit's foot from me and stuffs it in her tote bag. Awkwardly, Kwame and I separate and bookend Erzu and Renee.

We all walk on, and it's not long before we realize the jab

jabs around us this time are purely party revelers. There's joy of ritual and purpose in their eyes. They carry an excitement with them, a tradition that's been passed down to them, which they are proudly caretaking. They're focused, and almost in a trance, as they dance to the steel pan sounds. A few of them blow whistles to the beat or toss powder in the air.

We're still afraid, but the good kind of afraid. The Halloween and scary movie kind. Because of Erzu's powerful presence, for the moment we don't fear for our lives. And that's a good starting point, because we still have a Scotsman to locate.

When we finally reach the stately wonder that is the Grand Army Plaza arch, we stop under it for some peace. Renee and I pepper Erzu with compliments in English and in island Creole, thanking her for clearing our paths of jab jabs earlier.

"Looking beautiful, gyal," Renee tells her. "Have we told you that yet, sis?"

"Like a queen roaming her queendom," I add.

Erzu murmurs something in response as she makes herself comfortable next to Kwame's crouched figure. She sits, legs outstretched on the ground, and marvels at the arch ceiling.

"Yes, we are never alone," I translate, feeling like a boxing coach between rounds. "That's right, we're braver than we think. Thank you."

"Amen, we are," answers Renee, resting back against the

cool stone of the arch wall. "Even in the face of our terrifying fears."

I'm struck by that revelation and lean my shoulder on the wall to face her. "You saw it, too?"

"It was more like a feeling," shudders Renee. "Feeling Granny's spies all around, feeling judgment coming from them, feeling like I wanted to hide in shame."

My mighty lioness of a bestie deserves to hold her head way up, so it makes me want to fix whatever shame is haunting her. "Hide in shame?"

Renee fixes her lips to answer but freezes in silence.

I wait. What did she mean?

She finally gets her thoughts together and turns her head my way. "You know I live for new experiences, but I never imagined this . . ." Her voice trails off. "It's not really something I can talk about at Sunday school."

"Why? Don't people at your church be catching the spirit and speaking in tongues, too?"

I instantly feel bad about my response, because I get what Renee is saying. But it doesn't stop me from feeling slightly offended. Did Renee agree with what that woman on the van was saying about Vodou?

Kwame jumps up and coughs in response to my testy comeback.

"What about you?" Renee challenges Kwame. "Did *you* feel or see anything?"

The way she phrases her question brings to mind the presence of Grandma Rose I felt and heard this morning. I keep that to myself.

For Kwame, the question leaves his eyes scanning a specific memory. A shadow closes in on his face. But he doesn't share.

"Was it that bad?" I ask.

Renee chuckles. "Or maybe that embarrassing. Don't worry, we won't tell nobody you're a screamer."

Kwame playfully side-eyes us.

I can't help but titter along. It feels good to laugh with Renee. When she and I flash smiles at each other, I know the tension is squashed.

"So, boys shouldn't scream? Ah, I see sexism is alive and well here," sniffs Kwame. "Good to know."

"Okay, no more fighting," I laugh. "We're gonna need all of our heads together to get my aunt to the podcast on time, and I'm just so grateful to y'all that I'm not doing this alone."

After another minute of resting, we pull Erzu up and continue with our mission. We head through some of the checkpoints that have cropped up around J'Ouvert in the last few years as the celebration has gotten more fraught.

We finally come across a school bus, adorned with every flag of the Caribbean, plus the Progress Pride flag for good measure.

"Number forty-two," Renee says. "The driver said this is his friend's school bus number."

"Yo," says Kwame. "Either this dude is trying hard, or he really is some type of coexist brother."

I shrug. "I don't know. But if he can help us, I won't knock his hustle."

"Maybe he just wants to fit in," Renee offers.

"Hey!" A sunburned and sweaty White man with a broad smile and the reddest hair I've ever seen waves and bounds over to us. "I'm Scotty," he says in a thick, charming Scottish accent. "Are you the kids who just got off the dollar van?" he asks, and Kwame nods. "From the moment Ross called me and said you were here, I've been on the lookout for you."

Renee, Kwame, and I look at one another. *Ross?* Apparently, I'm not the only one who spent the entire dollar-van ride thinking the driver's name was Rasta when his name is Ross. Did we just collectively mishear the driver's name to stubbornly fit some stereotype in our mind?

Ugh. A new low.

"Sorry we're late," I say. "We got ambushed as soon as we got out of—er, Ross's—van."

Erzu already has her arm looped around Scottish Scotty's, and she's checking his biceps while making doe eyes at him. Renee looks torn between shock and awe.

"So, I heard you know a thing or two about spiritual malpractice," I say to Scotty while vigorously beckoning Erzu back to stand with us.

Scotty breaks his eye lock with Erzu and clears his throat

with an awkward laugh. "Sorry about your situation," he says. "But yes, I've seen it before. The Scottish tradition is one where mysticism has been in play for thousands of years. People respect it, even if they deny it's anything beyond lore and fairy tales."

That sounds familiar.

Face to the sky, he eyes a passing cloud as if he's expecting rain. "It's a magical day today. But with all these energies merging, there's no telling what's let loose."

Erzu seems to like being a topic of conversation. Grandma Rose would say she looks a lot like Vanna White, walking around Scotty and gesturing at invisible floating vowels.

"But at least you know you've got a positive spirit here," Scotty continues, smiling back at Erzu. "She's got a lot of energy!"

"Yeah, I feel like I'm babysitting a toddler sometimes," I groan. "But my friends are here to help, so I'm grateful."

"Don't worry," Scotty says. He frees himself from Erzu's gravitational pull, climbs the stairs of his bus, and goes to a hidden compartment next to the giant steering wheel. When he hops off, he hands something to me that looks like a handmade knit doll. "The poppet Ross said you needed," he explains.

I gape at it, grateful but curious. "Where did you get this?"

"When I was a kid, my nan used to make them and sell them as novelties. I was her little apprentice, and now I sell them online and people display them, use them, whatever."

"So, it's no different from, like, a New Orleans voodoo doll?"

Renee asks. "No shade," she adds quickly, and I know she really meant her question out of curiosity.

"You might have seen people on TV or in movies use something like this to do harm to their enemies," says Scotty, holding up the doll. "But there are more positive uses, too. You can pour love into the doll, send it encouragement. And in this case, this fetish would represent your aunt's spirit."

I clear my throat to keep the tears pricking my eyes at bay as I accept the handmade cloth figure and rub my thumb along its sewn edges.

Renee lays a comforting hand on my arm. "Could you maybe get her aunt back to normal, too?" she asks Scotty.

"I'm not the person you need to talk to about it," he answers earnestly.

"No offense, but obviously not," says Kwame. "This answer lies closer to home."

"No doubt, no doubt," says Scotty in understanding. "But if I can help you on your way . . . working as a bus driver on these streets for over a decade has taught me a thing or two about people and places in this fine borough of ours. Speaking of, I'm glad to give you all a ride. I'm heading back to the parade in a bit."

"We appreciate it," says Renee.

"Thank you, Scotty," I say, relieved. "That would be a huge help."

I pull out my phone and check the list again. So far, we've got the hex pouch, the rum, the mojo bone, and the fetish. Not bad.

Besides the high priestess, of course, we still need Florida Water, prayer beads, and the medicinal plant. Hmm.

"Scotty?" I say, glancing up at him. "Do you know where we can find a kind of plant used in spiritual ceremonies?"

Scotty tilts his head to one side. "Only person I can think of off the top of my head is Botany Bae. He knows so much about urban foraging. And he's here somewhere."

Renee glances nervously at me.

Botany Bae. "Wait," I say. "Uncle Rufus?"

Scotty nods. "He's the head of this nature group." He checks the time on his phone. "I'm sure you haven't missed him. He's actually leading a nature meditation walk through the park at ten, but he's never right on time." Scotty gestures toward the arch. "I think they're meeting over there. Feel free to come back to this bus when you're done."

Scotty smiles at us. Erzu waves to him and blows a kiss, which he promptly catches in one fist, blushing a little. Then he turns and heads inside his yellow bus.

"Meeting up with Uncle Rufus? Um, thanks but no thanks," Renee says quickly.

I'm intrigued, though. "A nature meditation walk?"

"Sounds more chill than what's happening in *these* streets," Kwame says.

"We've noticed this wasn't your favorite part," laughs Renee. She lets out a scream in the key of Kwame, making both Kwame and Erzu crack up.

I don't laugh, though. I'm too distracted by Renee's performance right now. Her whole faux scream is for sure funny, but it serves a purpose, too. She wants to distract us from talk of Botany Bae/Uncle Rufus. And I'm thinking it's not only because she doesn't want to get caught out here. Renee is the type who's willing to take risks to investigate a good story. It's almost as if she feels ashamed. Of my aunt? Of me? Of Vodou?

Maybe I'm overthinking this. And I've learned that things turn out the best if I'm *not* overthinking. Like the days I get the most compliments on my hair are the ones when I've hardly checked the mirror while combing it. If I'm distracted and chatting on the phone while cooking, the food actually tastes great.

I think about my mom's relationship with Tati Mimose. If I just stopped reading into it, maybe they'd find their way back to each other eventually.

"You okay?" Renee asks me.

"Yeah, *you?*"

She swats the air. "I'm ready to go back to the parade."

"Without the plant we need?" I ask her quietly. "Where else can we find it if not on this nature walk?"

She shrugs.

"Renee, it's okay if you head back without us. You don't have to do this, but I need to."

"What's it gonna *bee*, Re-*knee*?" Kwame asks like an annoying but lovable brother.

The worried look on Renee's face slowly melts away and she chuckles at the goofy rhyme in spite of herself. "Of course I'll stay." She glances at Erzu, who's doing a twirl around Kwame. "Who better can handle your aunt in this state?"

I smile, relieved. "You have been so amazing with her. I can't even tell you."

"Who knew that hours of living with my needy great-grandma would train me for this? That woman must be a child of this spirit because she don't act too different than Erzu. But to be honest, Erzu is easier to talk to."

She pauses and considers the thought as I watch Erzu spin Kwame around, ballroom-dancing style.

"Maybe this could teach me how to talk to my great-gran," Renee says finally. "I want to be closer to her, but sometimes it's so frustrating dealing with her diva ways that I stay away."

"You're lucky to be able to even know your great-gran," I say, hoping my voice is more soothing than goading.

When did I become one of those count-your-blessings people? But I don't rush to remind Renee that she's allowed to complain whenever she wants to. I'm too busy thinking that I've never met my own great-grandmother. And Grandma Rose's passing still feels so fresh. Her leaving cut short this next-level bond we were building. Just when she'd switched from calling me *baby girl* to *young lady*. She already started telling me certain things that she never used to tell me before.

Renee nods, and her breathy chuckle feels warm with empathy.

"Yeah, I know you're right. It's weird how we take things for granted when we do have them. But hopefully now I can work on being less annoyed the next time my gran breaks fly."

"I know you will," I say, holding up my pinky to her.

She interlaces her pinky with mine, and I take in the melodic sound of steel drums echoing out through the streets. This feels so quintessentially Labor Day. We're out here heralding the end of the summer in the only way we've ever known.

And then I spot him on a corner—Uncle Rufus. A small crowd is gathering around him, no doubt preparing for the nature walk.

"There he is," I tell Renee and Kwame, pointing. "Let's go."

Renee takes Erzu's hand and we all head over. When we're steps away from Uncle Rufus, Erzu stops to pick up a pair of maracas someone abandoned on the sidewalk. She begins shaking them side to side in the air, her hips swaying along.

Before I can ask her to drop the maracas, out of nowhere, a group of boys bum-rush us.

We're getting jumped!

CHAPTER EIGHT

We can't tell who's jumping us because they have black bandannas covering the lower halves of their faces. I count five teens. Hoping this is not an actual gang, I ball up my fists, ready to throw punches at whoever's coming at me.

But no one is.

The cluster of guys are all focused on Kwame, whose arms are restrained by two of the bulkier dudes.

"Yo, what the—" Renee shouts in shock.

"Get off him!" I roar.

Kwame grunts as he wrestles his arms free, but the soft punches he throws at the guys wouldn't harm a fly. "Y'all wrong for that!" he tells them, laughing.

The attackers laugh, too. Some of them pull down their bandannas and reveal their faces as they slap Kwame's hand and clap his back in a greeting.

"You know these fools?" I shout, winded. I pretend not to

recognize them, but I'd know those school hallway back claps anywhere.

"Unfortunately," Kwame answers with a smirk.

"They were ready, though—'*get off him*,'" one of the bulky dudes mimics my shout with a Hulk-angry face. Did I really look like that? They all snicker once more.

Kwame gives me that same shrug he gave me outside class that first day.

I glance over to see that Erzu is still shaking her maracas and dancing, totally oblivious to what happened to us. She's even been joined by a drummer. She'll have a full band if we don't move on soon.

"Roll with us," a clean-cut boy in sunglasses tells Kwame. "It's about to pop off."

"Wish I could, but can't," answers Kwame.

"C'mon, it's like that?" the boy says.

"Just can't right now, is all," Kwame says, the calm hum in his voice backing up his statement.

"It's cool," says a baby-faced bulky dude. He holds out the side of his fist for Kwame to bump. As soon as Kwame lifts his fist to give his friend dap, the clean-cut kid throws down a lit firecracker that goes off like a sonic boom.

Even though I see it happen, my body startles no differently than if I hadn't. Every person in the surrounding vicinity gasps, and a few even bolt. The group of boys takes off running, laughing as they go. Renee and I clutch each other, and we stumble toward

Erzu, a cursing Kwame following behind. My pounding heart doesn't settle until we reach Erzu and her drummer friend. They've stopped playing and are staring in the direction of the fleeing crowd.

No sooner do we all collect our breaths than event security zips in on a bike. The cycle's front wheel stops right at Kwame's toe and the woman leans over her handlebars to icily stare at Kwame.

"Why would you do that?" she asks.

"It wasn't him!" I say, upset.

"I'm asking *him*," she says without looking away from Kwame.

"I saw who threw it, and it wasn't this young man." An older man steps forward to speak up for Kwame.

It's Uncle Rufus. After all that knucklehead drama, it feels comforting to see him.

The security woman finally breaks from her Kwame glare. "Do you know him, Rufus?"

"He's with our botany tour. We're just about to get underway."

The cop eyes Kwame and then Uncle Rufus again before she sits back on her bike seat and slowly rolls away.

Once she's left the scene, we're left with Uncle Rufus, who stands with his hands clasped behind his back. He stares at us intently.

"Thank you," Kwame offers feebly.

Uncle Rufus continues staring suspiciously as we explain ourselves . . . badly. Erzu uses her adult-presenting privilege and stands at his side, wagging a finger at us.

"Those were some kids from school who ran into us," I snitch. "We didn't come here with them."

"N-not that we planned to come here," clarifies Renee. "Not at all. It was a last-minute necessity."

Uncle Rufus doesn't seem convinced and we know Renee is a goner. And then he drops his head in laughter.

"Care to join our nature walk tour?" he asks when he catches his breath.

We nod our heads, but I don't want to give him the idea that we're willing to take the whole tour. We don't have time for that.

"We're hoping you can help us find a ceremonial plant used in island rituals," I say, careful not to call out Vodou by name in case Uncle Rufus has any objections to that.

He eyes Erzu next to him and then looks back at me. "You mean like in Vodou?"

Renee wobbles a little like she might fall over.

"And don't look so frightened, child. No judgment here—your granny won't hear anything from me." He nudges Renee with an arm. "Young people, I think I know just the plant. We'll pass it early on in the tour."

"Thank you," Kwame says again in a small voice. He's obviously feeling guilty about his friends.

Renee's shoulders relax and we join the group of people following Uncle Rufus. Just a few yards from all the J'Ouvert jubilation and Grand Army Plaza's stone arch is the leafy green entrance to Prospect Park.

This is Brooklyn's Central Park, where I've met friends and family countless times for birthday picnics, summer strolls, and visits to the park's botanical gardens or zoo. I always feel calmer when I come here. Visiting this green space puts me in a reflective state of mind. As we enter the park, I look at the people lounging on the grass and on the benches. I make a mental note to come back here just to lie on a blanket and chill one weekend before it gets too cold out.

We head down a paved path, and the street traffic and celebrations are muffled. It feels like we've briefly left the city.

Uncle Rufus stops and turns to address his small gathering.

"Thank you for being here," he says warmly. He's bouncing on the balls of his feet the same way he did that day Renee and I saw him at the Junction. "Your soul has called out for this experience, and I'm honored to be the one to guide you through. I ask that as you all leave this space today, you thank the trees, the foliage, the greenery. Understand that they are welcoming you, and they are giving you so many benefits in return. We've long known that being out in nature has healing properties for us, all the way down to our souls and our minds and our bodies. And it's only in recent decades that science has supported that theory, but they have yet further to go."

It's nice to hear my thoughts echoed in Uncle Rufus's words. The natural world, just like the invisible world, feels very alive to me. It settles me and humbles me to remember that there's so much at work, both physically and spiritually, that keeps the universe universing. How often do people think about that?

But sometimes I wonder if I'm too curious about the mysteries of the universe. I don't have the Renee type of curiosity that leads to information that can help other people get on in the real world. My curiosity is the type that drew me closer to Tati Mimose's ceremony all those years ago. My curiosity got me possibly cursed, and it definitely caused a rift between two of my favorite people. My curiosity caused harm.

A gentle touch to my cheek makes me smile in spite of my mental spiral. I look at Erzu. Once she's sure I'm paying attention to her, she works her arms like she's popping and locking. And her whole body sways, which meets with the approval of people in our group. Another woman hypes her up.

Uncle Rufus acts like this is all perfectly normal, and his Caribbean TED Talk doesn't miss a beat.

"We know that we are in communion with J'Ouvert, an invigorating experience. It's an outlet our people in particular need—that space to express those chaotic energies that stir within all of us. And with the last few events being marred by violence from just a few unthinking people, we want to be here to support the spirit of J'Ouvert by counteracting negativity and sending out a powerful kind of love that would cancel out any harm. We will be sending out energy that serves as a force-field around our city. We know that this is the time for good things to flow in and bad things to flow out."

Uncle Rufus turns to gesture to some trees. Renee snaps a selfie, before taking pics of Uncle Rufus and the scenery he's introducing us to. I'm imagining she'll want to post about Botany Bae's guided tours. No doubt this post will be a #tbt or #fbf in case her granny catches wind that she was at the park during J'Ouvert.

"Letting the good flow in and the bad flow out. Sounds like exactly what we need," I whisper to Renee and Kwame. "Although I wouldn't characterize Erzu as *bad*."

"I wouldn't characterize Erzu as bad, either," Kwame answers. "Maybe just a bad dancer."

"Accurate," agrees Renee before she continues her documenting.

Kwame and I share a laugh, and Erzu looks back and mumbles something about Kwame to me. If I understand her correctly, she's making observations about him being different from the friends he surrounds himself with.

"Tell her no, we will not cut out the cutesy inside jokes," teases Kwame.

Mimose responds with more emphatic but incomprehensible mumbles.

"What's she saying about me?" he asks, suddenly catching on. "C'mon, I know you know."

Every time I think of just how much Kwame knows about me and my family, I get embarrassed all over again. But I translate for him anyway.

"The spirit thinks you're way nerdier than you pretend to be."

"Hmmm . . ." he says. "Why do you think that is?"

I respond with his trademark shrug

"Oh, I get it." He walks backward, eyeing me with amusement. "A shrug, because I've done that before . . . to you."

"Ah, I'm impressed you were paying attention." I smirk.

He smiles back. "I do that from time to time."

"Oh yeah, you're in-Pheme-ous for that."

I have to keep my swooning in check. I should be paying attention to Uncle Rufus.

Kwame turns back around and walks in step with me. "How is it you can translate what Erzu says?"

This time, my shrug isn't ironic. I don't know. Am I really a manbo, as Juste said? Does my ability have something to do with what happened at that ceremony with Mimose when I was nine? I have no answers, so I focus back on Uncle Rufus.

Right now, he's stopped walking and has placed a hand on a tree. "We are not here to recklessly take from Mother Nature," he tells the group with his village elder vibe. "We have to do things with intention. The trees speak to each other through an extensive system right underneath your feet. And who can say for sure they don't sense your heart and your motivations? So use your breath to clear out anything that could be blocking you from fully engaging with this experience."

I draw in and let out a deep breath, smelling the fragrant leaves.

"Did you say that tree is talking to us?" a young man in the group asks, digging a finger in his ear as if he heard wrong.

"There's lots of ways to communicate," Uncle Rufus replies. "You're always in communication with something at all times. Whether you are aware of it is another story. You have a relationship with every space you travel in. The same is true with nature. Even on city streets, there's greenery pushing through the cracks. As you learn more about identifying herbs and plants, you may find that sidewalk sprouts carry as much value as anything you can find in the park. It's all related. So why not start that conversation by becoming familiar with these plants growing all around us?"

"That's . . . interesting," the man answers.

"Yes it is. So let's keep an open mind."

I find myself nodding. Everything Uncle Rufus is saying feels like confirmation of the persistent, mysterious thoughts that keep me company from time to time. It's that sixth-sense feeling, like I *can* communicate on another level if I want to.

But *do* I want to converse with the spiritual realm? It's not something I asked for, and I'm not sure I see it as a gift. Being this person who talks to sprits could make me an outsider, and I'm not sure how I'd handle that. I'm not the confident beauty that Tati Mimose is, nor do I have Renee's powerful voice or mighty journalistic pen. I'm just a girl who sometimes imagines the cosmos, occasionally hears her grandma, and daydreams about being kissed.

My phone dings. It's my mom checking on me again.

Where'd you go off to? I figured you'd be back by now.

This is phase one, going on phase two of Margo's worry scale. I feel awful that I've made my mom stressed, but I don't respond yet.

If Mom knew I was with Mimose—if she knew what Mimose had gotten me into—I know exactly what she would say: *Mimose cares more about herself than anyone in the world.*

Renee sees the look of anguish on my face and whispers, "Is it your mom?" She knows me too well.

I nod. "I'm not going to answer yet," I whisper back, stashing my phone away.

Uncle Rufus is leading our group toward a grassy field up ahead.

"Why are you avoiding your mom?" Kwame asks me softly as we walk.

How can I explain the pressures I've been under not to hang with Mimose?

"My mom thinks my aunt will only expose me to some wacky spiritual element and that I'll be in a bind for it," I say.

Kwame blank-stares at me, and the awareness of our exact predicament sinks in.

Erzu turns to me and Kwame. She distracts us by making gestures that strongly suggest the two of us hold hands. Renee catches her meaning and bites down on her laugh. Erzu is totally shipping me with Kwame, and it's making us Black-folk blush.

We've reached the grassy field, and Uncle Rufus is now urging everyone to kick off our shoes and connect with Mother Earth. Renee kicks off her sneakers and Erzu slips off her sandals. I watch as the two of them frolic around on the grass.

I can feel Kwame glance at me. I'm not sure if he's trying to make eye contact because I'm too flustered to check. "How about it?" he asks me.

My smile is a reflex. "Yeah, sure."

We kick off our sneakers. Kwame takes my hand in his, and I can feel my face temperature switch to broil. He leads me to a picturesque spot, past a hipster couple from the tour who are chasing each other barefoot in the grass.

"Mother Earth!" Kwame shouts playfully. "Mind if we make ourselves at home?"

"Come on in!" I answer in my best Mother Earth goddess voice, which ends up sounding like a wannabe opera diva.

We both laugh. Kwame plops down and then lies flat in the grass like he's on a living room recliner.

"Ahhh, " he says, shielding his eyes from the sun. "This is nice. Come try it."

I circle around him, then sit down in the grass and lie back with my body pointing the opposite way, so that only our heads are side by side.

This *is* nice. The tickly grass is warm against my neck and the sun blankets my face. For once, Kwame and I don't crack jokes, but instead fall into silence.

The closeness of his cheek—of his lips—makes it hard to speak.

It would take nothing to angle toward him. If we both turned toward each other even slightly, our lips would almost touch.

Would that count as a kiss?

Wondering this throws off my breathing. I pretend like I'm taking in an Uncle-Rufus-recommended deep breath.

"Let's move on!" Uncle Rufus calls then, breaking me out of my thoughts. Kwame and I reluctantly get to our feet, find our sneakers, find Erzu and Renee, and rejoin Uncle Rufus. The tour continues, with Uncle Rufus talking more about the plants around us.

Erzu seems to fully embrace whatever energy Uncle Rufus says nature is serving. She sways her arms in the air, does a few spins, and touches trees in passing. She smiles more than I've seen her smile this whole day. The group smiles back at her, clearly enjoying her presence, and some of them join in with her flapping-arms dance.

I study Erzu/Mimose, feeling a mix of fondness and worry. If I'm being real with myself, I guess I've always had a low-level worry for my aunt. She comes across so independent, and she puts up a good show of flamboyantly marching to the beat of her own drum. But in her quiet moments when she didn't think anyone was looking, I was the one still closely watching and listening. Pretty soon, I developed a pitch-perfect ear for my aunt's rhythms, and I started to detect that her beats would skip or grow hollow when my mother would make a snide remark about Vodou practices.

Mimose has lost her mom, her one solid cheerleader besides me, and I know this hits her when she's alone. Tati Mimose doesn't show it because she's expected to be so many things for so many people. Her Instagram comments alone are filled with so many stories about how she's influenced people or how she's inspired them to go deeper, do better, and be better. She encourages her followers to believe in themselves and step out of their comfort zones, all without proselytizing or pushing Vodou on anyone. She presents it as a part of her personal journey, and I think most people view her like a cultural ambassador rather than a Vodou peddler.

My aunt's online platform has exploded, and today is supposed to be a huge win for her. It's hard to believe everything could blow up in her face if we don't do something about Erzu.

But right now, she is free of those concerns and dancing her heart out.

"Yes, let it ride through you," encourages Uncle Rufus. "You could be a vessel of something to flow through."

My eyebrow hitches at the mention of vessels. Could all this flow help my aunt flow right back into the pilot seat again? But no. It's just Erzu being Erzu. I feel myself tense up again. We need to get that medicinal plant—and fast.

Almost as if he's heard my thoughts, Uncle Rufus stops. What looks like a pile of oddly shaped shrubbery I wouldn't give a second glance is exactly what he reaches for. A memory I'd long hidden sprouts up clearly in mind: my grandmother picking through a bush in this same way. It hits me then: Grandma Rose was a forager. She wanted to make healing oils to use on her skin, so I remember her taking me to the park and doing exactly what Uncle Rufus is doing now.

"And here's a medicinal plant valued for what some believe is the ability to spiritually cleanse."

Clearly missing the part where we're trying to evict her, Erzu traipses over to the plant. She runs a languid hand through the waxy shrub as if she's playing chimes.

Uncle Rufus's gold tooth glimmers at Erzu. "Looks like someone respects the power of this herb. Normally during a ceremony, you would drench these leaves with Florida Water and then pat them against a person's skin. I'm no expert, but I've seen it done that way before," he says. "The land plays a huge role in spiritual practices of all kinds. In Vodou, a tree makes for the perfect poto-mitan, or pillar, around which a ceremony is conducted."

Was that a poto-mitan at the ceremony I witnessed those years ago? I think of the fiery basin setup in my living room, and wonder if that was the center Uncle Rufus is talking about.

Uncle Rufus turns over a leaf so he can rub a thumb across its hairy underside. Renee leans in closer to take a shot of his dark brown hands shining under the morning sun. As he speaks and explains its medicinal value, its purpose, and how it should be used, I can't get over how much of a natural he is at this, pun intended. So natural with nature.

Who knew the old dude standing on the Junction would be the person we'd both least and most want to run into at J'Ouvert?

When he's done giving his presentation, I ask Uncle Rufus if we can have some leaves of that plant. He nods and gently plucks some leaves, handing them over. I place the leaves in Renee's tote bag. A little piece of beautiful Prospect Park.

"Be safe, and best of luck," Uncle Rufus tells us.

It's time to go. We thank Uncle Rufus for the tour, and Renee, Kwame, and I—tugging Erzu along—head for one of the park's exits so we can meet up with Scottish Scotty and his bus. As we're going, Tati Mimose's phone rings. I dig it out from her pouch and see her intern's name on the screen.

"Hi, Jovita—it's Cicely," I answer.

"Where's your aunt?" Jovita sounds pressed. "I need to go over a few details with her before the interview."

"We're headed to the parade route now," I say. I realize I can't keep avoiding Jovita. In fact, maybe she'll help us out of this mess.

I don't go into specifics, but agree to meet Jovita at the Franklin Avenue station.

After I hang up Mimose's phone, I check mine for the list. We're doing okay. We have the hex pouch, the rum, the mojo bone, the fetish, and now the plant. We just need to find Florida Water, prayer beads, and, of course, the priestess.

We need to move quick. But on our way out of the park, we remember to thank the trees.

CHAPTER NINE

By the time Scottish Scotty's yellow bus rumbles to a stop near Eastern Parkway, it's already ten forty-five. We thank Scotty and hop off on a side street. The air is charged with electric excitement; the parade will be kicking off soon. Renee, Kwame, Erzu, and I join the crowd, moving as one toward the parade intersection.

It's wild to think that when I woke up this morning, my mission was all about the parade, my aunt, and Papash. Papash's image was so vivid in my mind, I could almost take a selfie with it. Now that image has started to get fuzzy. I'm not letting it fade to black just yet. If there's a chance I still can meet Papash, I'll jump on it. But for now, my mission is about disaster management.

Still, it's hard not to get swept up in the sense of anticipation. The lifeblood of the streets is pulsing. It's like we are all being cradled and rocked by the thumping island music playing from every speaker. The buildings lining the streets seem taller, more upright, as if they're breathing in our pride.

The crowd's excitement peaks when we reach Eastern Parkway, the broad avenue that hosts the parade. People are nabbing spots on the sidelines where they can watch the action. When the explosion of color, aroma, and sound hits, my senses go into overdrive.

The parkway is lined with metal barricades, and bright flags hang from windows and streetlamps. Under colorful umbrellas, food vendors serve marinated meats, to wash down with sorrel beer, ginger beer, and cane juice. And people are dressed to party at this celebration of Caribbean life. Everyone who understood the assignment wears clothes accented with their island nation flags. Some girls I spot wear actual flags as tube tops, headbands, or capes; homies let their flags hang from their belt loops or out their back pockets. Honduras, Saint Vincent, Barbados, Montserrat, Bermuda, and, a personal favorite, Guyana, are all showing out, and we love to see it.

Every small detail has been planned and pored over to perfection. I see peekaboo bodysuits and strappy sandals that crisscross up the thighs. All around us are brown faces speckled with shiny gold dust and sparkly gemstones. Everyone is strutting with what they are repping, and it's a glorious sight.

I remember the tablescape my parents created for me this morning. Today, it feels like everyone's birthday. Like all of us here have been born under the same star sign, connected by shared characteristics and experiences. We celebrate ourselves and one another.

"I see you, Panama!" Renee calls. I turn to admire a supremely coordinated group of Panama-flag-draped girls sitting on the barricades, and I beam at them with pride. Then I notice a familiar face up ahead.

"Jamaican Beauty!" I call out to my neighbor who's standing at the curb. I know she's here representing the Brooklyn borough president's office. She waves back at me, but she's so distracted by the group of overdressed politicians she's with, she doesn't stop to chat long enough to notice anything strange about topsy-turvy Mimose. That's a relief.

Every year, Eastern Parkway is the site of many impromptu reunions. The attendance numbers are in the hundreds of thousands, and as Renee noted, lots of people fly in from far-flung places. Yet it's guaranteed locals will bump into other locals and catch up on the spot.

I watch as the girl walking in front of me yanks her friend by the arm to keep her from running into an upcoming streetlamp. It reminds me of how I usually have to keep Renee on track when she's looking at her phone.

And it makes me wonder: What happens spiritually when two people end up walking on opposite sides of a pole? Is a tether severed? How does it repair? And how far does that tether reach? No couple, no BFF pair, spends every waking minute together, right?

I glance at Renee. Usually, she's dead set against separating when she's walking with me, her gyal pal. But right now, she's obviously not wondering about poles and tethers. Instead she seems shifty-eyed, like she's on high alert and worried she'll run into someone else she knows. At this point, everyone on Eastern Parkway looks familiar, so I don't know how long she can keep this worrying up.

And on the next block, we do run into someone—but this time it's Jovita. And she sees us even before we spot her. My aunt's intern is nothing if not efficient and super sharp. The girl is only three years older than us, but she's already in her second year at Brooklyn College and a marketing genius. Tati Mimose's social media posts got a lot more frequent when Jovita came on board, and her followers grew a lot faster. The sponsors have taken notice and piled on. I know all these things because my aunt sings Jovita's praises every chance she gets.

Jovita's wearing black shorts and a sleeveless denim button-down that she's tied at the waist, but somehow she gives the impression that she's wearing a suit. She wears a Jamaica flag pin like a politician would. It's pinned on her shirt near her heart.

"Jovita! Thank goodness. It's been a day," I say before introducing her to Renee and Kwame. Erzu wraps Jovita in an embrace.

Jovita warmly hugs Erzu back, even though I'm sure it's not the customary greeting Jovita gets from Mimose.

"Hey there, Mimose." Jovita smiles. "I see you're swept up in the island love. But you're cutting it close. You gotta be getting over to the podcast stage soon."

The entire ride over here, I've been thinking of a gentle way to break the news to Jovita. She's no doubt worked so hard to land this big interview for my aunt.

Erzu looks at Jovita and smiles dreamily at her, touching her hair and patting her on the back.

"Are you okay?" Jovita asks her. "You don't seem like yourself at all."

When my aunt sways from side to side instead of answering, Jovita looks back at me for an explanation.

I wince. "Well, technically, she's not . . . herself."

Jovita watches as my aunt takes Kwame's hand and leads him in a quickstep that looks very *Dancing with the Stars*. Renee laughs, grabbing her phone to document.

"What do you mean?" Jovita asks. "What's going on?"

I say, "There's been a mishap. The client she went to read cards for, this guy Juste? He wanted a ceremony. And when my aunt refused him that request, he took matters in his own hands and conjured this spirit of Erzu to take command of Mimose's body."

There you have it. It sounds bonkers to say it out loud.

Jovita's eyes widen. "No way. Someone named Juste emailed Mimose's account after I talked to you earlier. He said he's looking to give her something of hers she left at his place. Her tarot cards. They're her favorite set, I know, so I told him that I'd be meeting you here. So he should be here any minute."

I freeze.

"What?" Renee asks loudly enough to turn Kwame's and Erzu's heads mid-spin.

Jovita looks a little panicked. "I'm sorry. Unfortunately, that's how it went down. If I'd known what happened, I would've never told him to meet me."

"Jovita, that man is intense," I say, thinking of the worn shoulders on his life-sized Tom Cruise cutout.

"Oh no," frets Jovita. "And today of all days."

"It's okay. You couldn't have known," I tell her.

Jovita continues her laments as if she didn't hear me. "Do you think she's in a good place? When can we get her back? I promised the podcast producers a top-tier interview. Mimose came up with an amazing list of questions."

"Jovita, Jovita." A winded Kwame walks over to try and help me calm her down as Renee leads Erzu away for a little distracting stroll.

I hold up my hands, palms out. "Don't worry, we're handling it. That's why we're looking for a priestess. We'll get this reversed," I say. *At least, I hope so.*

Kwame and I glance at each other and it's understood that we have to move from this spot to avoid encountering Juste. I gesture for Jovita to lead the way.

"Right," says Jovita, bouncing back to corporate form. "Last I heard, Nuna's chiropractor float will be near the front of the parade. I'll text you the podcast location and I will meet you there."

"Sounds like a plan," I say, though I'm not looking at Jovita. I'm completely mesmerized by the pretty crystals lined up at a nearby vendor's table. Galactic and gleaming, they remind me of the star travel dreams of my childhood.

The vendor notices my interest and hooks me in with her sales pitch. "That one is the black tourmaline. Puts you right back into your body. Very grounding."

Puts you right back into your body. With those words, my eyes flicker away from the stone to the speaker. She kind of resembles the smooth stones on display. Her long, straight hair and skin are dark and shiny, and her face is all smooth angles.

"Would you like to hold one and take a moment to get grounded?" the vendor asks.

"Sure," I say.

"Really, Cicely?" asks Kwame. Jovita moves in closer to see what I'm fussing over.

I look at him and give him the same shoulder shake he's given me. A dimple forms in Kwame's cheek when he recognizes the gesture. He nods. *Touché.*

Before handing me the stone, the vendor grabs a bottle of . . . Florida Water! I stare wide-eyed as she adds the solution to a cloth, which she uses to rub down the stone.

I gasp and point. "Are you selling those?"

"Yes, all crystals are for sale."

"No, I mean that Florida Water."

"Oh, this? No, but I always keep a few bottles on hand so I

can wipe the energetic residue off each crystal as they change hands."

"I'll buy one off you," I say like someone ready to haggle at an open market.

The vendor has barely told me the price before a man's voice drowns hers out.

"Hey, I know you!" he hollers.

I turn around and my stomach drops. It's Juste. He's changed outfits since I last saw him—now he has on these extra-baggy, extra-long denim shorts straight from a '90s Kris Kross video set.

"Um . . . Cicely?" Kwame says before I can react to Juste. "Where is Mimose dragging Renee off to?"

I look to where Kwame is pointing. To my parents' booth!

CHAPTER TEN

"Quick, let's go," I gasp, practically tossing the dollar at the vendor and snatching the bottle of Florida Water. I turn to face Kwame and Jovita. "If my mom sees Mimose in this condition, she will shut down this whole parade. All of Eastern Parkway will have to pack up and go home."

Juste is still on our tail and getting closer, judging by the reach of his voice. "I'm talking to you!" he shouts at our backs.

Kwame puffs out his chest and starts to walk toward Juste. I grab his arm. "It's not worth it . . . unless you're up on your Tom Cruise trivia," I say.

"Huh?"

"Never mind."

We cross into a mob of people to lose him, but Juste apparently knows how to make his way through a crowd. He's probably been practicing this in carnivals past, way before we were born.

Thankfully, we're nimbler. So we duck, cut, and run.

Jovita is light on her feet, weaving with us through the crowd and looking back every now and then to report Juste's proximity.

"Mimose! I just need a little bit of your time!" he bellows.

But I'm more concerned with where Erzu is heading. That mischief of a spirit is looking for trouble by still making a beeline for my parents.

Thankfully, Renee manages to rein in Erzu, and stops her before they reach the Port-au-Princesse booth. The two are now standing on the corner across the street from us.

Before I can cross the street, a trio of performers on stilts appears. The stilt walkers are mesmerizing for sure. Dressed in bright, silky island ensembles, they hop, wine, and sashay down the street to a soca hit list thumping from a nearby boom box.

I catch flashes of Renee and my aunt between the hard-working performers, but we can't make it across to them. This feels like trying to cross the street during the New York City Marathon. When my family and I cheered on runners passing through Bed Stuy, the only way we were able to cross that road was to head underground into a subway station and come up on the other side of the street. Here, crossing between stilt walkers would be riskier than getting mowed down by a marathoner. My overactive brain conjures up the sensation of being clamped between tall stilts. It's not a pleasant one. Imagining the domino effect that would have on the whole troupe of high-rise performers is even worse. I would go viral for the wrong reason.

Kwame's gentle squeeze on my hand welcomes me back from my stilt-dominoes viral-video alternate reality.

Our slowdown has left the perfect opening for Juste, who comes up right behind us.

"What do you want?" I shout at him.

"I want what's mine," Juste answers, a whiny note in his voice. "She has a job to do and she hadn't done it. And I'm not gonna stop until I get it."

"Maybe if I reschedule his reading that'll satisfy him?" says Jovita.

I shake my head.

Nothing can be resolved this way because there's no use in arguing with someone who is that relentless. I pick up the pace, heading straight for my aunt and Renee. The crowds between us have thickened, and they're farther away now.

"Stay back," Kwame tells Juste.

"This got nothing to do with you, boy." Clearly assuming that Kwame is Haitian, Juste hurls Creole insults at him, not knowing that Kwame doesn't understand a word.

We are out of breath for running under this blazing sun. Jovita coughs the cough of the asthmatic person. I know that sound because I'm a sufferer, too. I hope she has enough water in that corporate-looking backpack of hers. I squint my eyes at the glint of silver I see peeking between the flaps, because did homegirl bring a laptop to the Labor Day Parade?

Oh, God help us. I say a silent prayer.

"Pitite Margo! Pitite Margo!" an older woman calls out, and holds out her arm to stop me from running past her. I'd recognize that fabulous two-tone wig anywhere. It's Solange, one of the restaurant's few regular customers. "Where is your mother's booth? I've been looking for it."

I don't mean to be rude, but I can't stop. Unless I can? Kwame gestures to Juste's sudden slowdown. Something about this woman has got Juste masking his hunt.

"Whoo, this is the best spot." Solange lets loose a peal of laughter, and it sounds like wind chimes. "I'm seeing everyone I know out here today. You're in a rush, darling, but I just want to know, where is your mother's setup?"

"Oh, that's no problem," I say, pointing two o'clock across the street, showing her exactly where she can get a tasty Port-au-Princesse lunch. Through the smoke from the grill, I can just make out the back of my mom's head nodding as she chats to a customer. Kwame and Jovita take this moment to catch their breath. Juste is lurking a few yards away, clearly waiting until we finish our conversation.

The woman thanks me and then happens to glance in Juste's direction. "Yes, Lord, so many people I know are passing through. I know that young man, too. Juste, is that you?"

Solange beckons Juste over like he's five years old, and he has no choice but to obey the older woman.

She points right at his Karl Kani top. "Listen, I wanted to hire you out, I have an event coming up. How much do you charge to DJ on a Friday night?"

That's our cue. Kwame, Jovita, and I turn and flee. I'm relieved, but my heart is still racing.

And I look ahead and see that Erzu is plowing toward my parents' booth again, Renee running behind her. Oh no.

There's only one solution. "Can you please take my aunt away while I talk to my parents?" I whisper to Kwame and Jovita. "Just for five minutes."

"Okay, but make it quick," Kwame says.

I look at Kwame and consider whether to tease back that I don't follow orders from him, but there's no time for that.

Mom, Dad, and Adeline are busy keeping the fires burning under the food of the grill. Everything smells amazing.

I see it all happening in agonizing slow motion. Mimose gets there before me and is about to step in front of a customer. But as my mom is about to look up and see her sister, Juste's shout captures my mom's attention.

"Erzu? Erzu, you're still here!"

My mom looks his way and spots me. She waves, and I do a goofy dance in greeting to keep her eyes locked on me while Kwame and Jovita calmly take Erzu by her arms and lead her away. I run over to Renee, playing it like the two of us have been together this whole time.

Mom laughs at my antics. "There she is! Babe, look who's

back," she calls to my dad. "We've been wondering when you'd get here."

"Birthday girl!" says Daddy, smiling big.

I glance back at Renee and flash her a look of panic, and she gives me her *no worries* head shake.

"Erzu!" Juste is still shouting, now following my aunt, Kwame, and Jovita. Even with Juste's loudmouth popping off, I see that Renee is right. Between the crowd and Erzu being used as a decoy, Juste has cleared out of this location, and I have a feeling Kwame and Jovita will outpace him again and double back quickly.

Still, my mom and dad looked piqued by Juste's shouting. I kiss my parents' cheeks, then shake my head. "What kind of a name is Erzu?" I ask, trying to play it cool. "Hipsters taking over Brooklyn, amiright?"

Mom taps a finger to her forehead, to her chest, and finally to each shoulder, in the sign of the cross. "That name sounds close to a name I know of."

I freeze. Does she recognize the name of the spirit?

"Hi, Mr. and Ms. Destin," Renee greets them, mercifully taking the attention off me.

"Hello, darling." Mom waves from behind her decked-out table. I love our Haitian flag tablecloth. All the utensils and napkins match, too. Port-au-Princesse is giving panache with quality street food and I wish more people would appreciate it. "Where have you two been?" Mom asks me.

"Oh, like I said, I ran into Renee, and we ran into other people we knew and just hung out for a little bit," I say quickly.

"Oh, okay, I figured it was something like that," says Daddy. I watch as he unleashes a billowy cloud of mouthwatering aroma when he opens the grill. He grimaces the moment the heat smacks him in the face. "But next time, why don't you keep us updated? Text your mom or dad and let us know."

"I'm sorry," I say, meaning it. "And, well, you know, I was thinking," I go on, improvising on my feet. "It's probably better that I don't stay here. I could be more of a help if I am out spreading the word about your location. People have been asking, like that woman who always comes in wearing the two-toned Cruella de Vil wig? I just saw her."

Mom purrs. "Aw, that Solange is the best—so lovely all the time. God bless her." She presses down on the word *that* like she's singling out this Solange versus any other Solange she knows. And I can think of at least three others—it's a popular Haitian grandmother name.

"I'm sure God has," I say.

I see my mom look quietly from me to Renee, as if trying to read the subtext. My only prayer is that Renee keeps those flashing, breaking-news eyes of hers neutral. The last thing we need is for my mom to find Renee's face extra readable right now.

I glance over and the opposite is true. Renee's alert notifications are turned off. In fact, she looks like she's just been injected with Botox. There's not a twitch in her face, or even a blink . . . which probably tells my mom that something's up.

"Are you sure everything is okay? Mom asks.

"Yeah, all good," I blurt. "We saw a couple of cute boys, so that's probably why we're acting a little off."

What am I saying?

"Oh, I see you waste no time. As soon as your calendar strikes fifteen you're already out, trying to find a dream boy, huh? Well, slow down, missy. There's no rush. And that goes for the both of you."

"We know, we know." I wince. "But, Mom, I'll just grab a few of our flyers to help spread the news about this booth. If Renee and I go down to the parade, we can hand them out." I reach behind the booth and find the colorful leaflets in the paper products bag. "Here they are!"

"That's my girl, always thinking ahead," Daddy says, wiping his face with a hand towel.

"Well, you know, it's the way I was raised." I smile.

"Margo, it's our girl's birthday and she's working, so it's fine with me if it's fine with you," Daddy says.

"All right, but just as long as you text us and let us know your status and when you're coming back," Mom says. "And I'll be asking customers if they were given a flyer."

I give her a "No doubt. I got you, Mom," followed by a "Smells good." And add in a "By the way, everything looks good, too."

That's like the fifth compliment, so I think *I'm* good.

My parents hit me back with "All right, see you later," backed by their go-to "Be safe!"

"Bye, Mr. and Ms. Destin." Renee finally speaks up, and her face at last moves into a smile.

Our work done, I mumble to Renee, "Let's go."

We both add a happy-go-lucky bounce to our gait in case my mom is watching. I still think she suspects something.

Our conversation, meanwhile, is anything but happy-go-lucky.

"Can you imagine what would happen if your aunt keeps Papash waiting?" asks Renee.

"I can't imagine. Especially because I know she'd never forgive herself."

"What if they ask *us* do the interview with Papash instead? Would you be able to?" Renee asks.

"Me? Not without sounding like a complete fool rapping 'Act a Fool' on April Fool's Day," I sputter. "I mean, you're the journalist. You could definitely play it off."

"Not without passing out every time he looks into my eyes. Have you seen his eyes?"

"My eyes?" Kwame with the supersonic hearing teases when we join him, Erzu, and Jovita on the next street. He points to his handsome face. "You're talking about these eyes?"

I play like he's being a pest as I step around him and loop my arm around Erzu's, when really I'm swooning inside. "So, real quick, y'all . . . I got the Florida Water, so that means, besides the priestess, all we need are the rosary beads."

167

Jovita shrugs. "That's an easy one. My parents have tons of rosaries at home. I live right nearby, so I can go get them and text you when I'm on my way back."

That's perfect. "Thank you."

"Now all we gotta do is find a priestess dressed as a butterfly," says Renee as Jovita hurries off.

Kwame checks the time on his phone. "If we do that in the next half hour, we still have time to get your aunt de-possessed before the interview."

I nod like a self-important action hero from a bad '90s blockbuster. I don't know any other way to react when you've just been chased by a naughty-by-'90s villain.

"Let's find this float!" I declare.

CHAPTER ELEVEN

I stand with Kwame, Renee, and Erzu on the corner of Eastern Parkway, waiting excitedly for the first float to appear. Renee has got Kofi on her phone on FaceTime; Kwame's kid brother is camped out on the roof of his building, keeping watch for the floats, too.

Maybe it's the relief of having the green light from my parents, or the relief of not presently being chased by Juste, but I'm finally letting myself celebrate Caribbean Christmas.

The West Indian Day Parade is happening. Now. In this moment. And I am with my best friend. I'm also with the boy who, if I'm being honest, makes me feel things I haven't felt before.

And I'm finally with my aunt—sort of. One of my favorite people on the planet, even if she's not herself today. But it's parade time and I'm where I'm meant to be.

People who have been to Trinidad's or Brazil's

world-famous carnivals, or even to the one in Haiti, have said those are bigger and wilder than Brooklyn's more structured, barricaded affair. My parents have been to the ones in Toronto and London, and say those have different vibes altogether. But here in Brooklyn, we do Carnival our way. The main thing is, if you're going to join, you bring your flag. Guarantee, every MC who shouts from the trucks will hype the crowd to "wave your flag in the air."

And it's happening already. People jump up and wave as one big unit. It's lucky Kwame just bought a Pan African flag from a curbside vendor. I help him tie the red, black, and green flag around his arm. Renee throws up her Trinidad and Tobago flag, and Erzu cheers. Those who aren't jumping wine their hips and bounce along as the first truck, Grenada, starts to make its way down the street.

The moment the floats arrive is always thrilling. The eighteen-wheeler truck bearing its load of speakers on full blast slowly creeps up the Parkway, its presence felt and heard long before it is ever seen. When it finally comes into view, it's led by tens of mas camps. These masquerade crews are dressed in the most elaborately costumed wonders you've ever laid eyes on. They *are* the carnival, and they will not stop giving energy to the crowd the entire time they dance their way down de Parkway.

I take in a gulp of this moment and my tongue tries to remember the taste of it. "This is so dope. I can't believe we're all hanging out at the Labor Day Parade together."

Kwame looks at me and smiles. "I didn't see today going down like this."

"That's an understatement," I laugh, glancing at a dancing Erzu.

"No, I mean I was just planning on watching from home and not really participating," Kwame says.

I shake my head. "As long as I have a pulse, I don't know how a person cannot be affected by all this energy out here."

"Yeah, don't get me wrong, I love it. It's just, I didn't want to be in the mix this year."

"If now's not your time to be in the mix, then when?" asks Renee.

Renee is holding up her phone and Kofi's face greets us from her screen. "He just wanted to avoid seeing the Saint Lucian mas camp that's dressed up like Black Panther this year. He wanted to rock with them so bad, but he didn't think he perfected his wine enough to join them."

Renee pretends to look stunned. "You don't know how to wine?"

Kwame grunts at his brother. "Nowhere in rooftop report did we mean reporting my personal business, though."

I laugh. "Is that even a little bit true?"

"It's not," mumbles Kwame.

"Yeah, I caught him dancing in front of the mirror once," Kofi cuts in. "He tried to play it off, but he had on a wine tutorial on YouTube, so he can't deny that. Don't be ashamed. Maybe that camp will accept you next year—despite your lack of talent and lack of shared culture. He's not even true Saint Lucian."

"That's not true," Kwame says. "Well, it's true I'm not Saint Lucian, but that's not why I never tried out."

"So, what's the reason, then?" I ask.

He swats the air and I imagine he wishes he could mush Kofi's face instead. "Just something I never took to the next level."

"Told ya, no culture," says Kofi.

"You do know that we're from the same bloodline," says Kwame.

"Oh, I know our people have culture," Kofi clarifies. "We are the definition of culture. Just testing YOU."

"This kid." Kwame takes a playful jab at Renee's screen.

Kofi deftly changes the subject. "So y'all are waiting on a butterfly float, right?" he asks. "I don't see it yet from where I am."

"Okay, call us back if you spot it," Renee tells Kofi, and he nods before hanging up. I can tell Kwame is relieved.

Renee checks something else on her phone. "I was reading about the parade route, and the chiropractor float should be right after the Saint Kitts and Nevis one."

"Green, black, and red, with the diagonal black bar and white stars," I say. My mom has pointed out the flag to me only a gazillion times. She loves to remind me that the parents of my namesake, the great actor Cicely Tyson, hailed from Saint Kitts and Nevis.

"I'm excited to see this butterfly priestess," Renee says. "I looked up her mas camp, and apparently her costume has been years in the making. Some are speculating that it may be one of the largest costumes in Carnival history. Her butterfly wingspan alone is supposed to be so ginormous, it's on wheels."

"Whoa," I say.

Blown away by all these new details, I've almost forgotten a literal obstacle we have to hurdle to get to the queen of butterflies: the security barriers lining the perimeter of the parade route. We're still on the sidewalk with the spectators when we need to be *in* the streets to talk to the priestess.

"I have an idea," I tell Kwame and Renee, and I gesture for them to follow me to the two cops patrolling the next intersection. My mom once told me that in years past, it wasn't too hard to break the barrier and join the procession. But now they've beefed up the security.

"All right, Erzu, we need you to act as normal as possible," whispers Renee.

"Either that or let Mimose hop in the driver's seat for a minute just to help you maneuver out this tight spot. And then I promise you can take over once that's done," I say to Erzu.

She mumbles something I miss, but her cackle afterward lets me know she ain't giving up that steering wheel.

I shrug. "It was worth a try."

I smile and approach the younger of the two cops, hoping she'll be easier to convince. I pretend that we, Mimose's handlers, are speaking on her behalf.

"Hi, this is my aunt who is interviewing Papash on the podcast stage today," I say.

Unmoved, the woman shakes her head and points to send us back where we came from. My heart sinks.

Then the older cop speaks up. "Oh, I recognize her," he says, nodding at Erzu. "Isn't she the one who does card readings online?"

"Yes, that's her," I say, perking up.

"I've been following her for a little bit now, but every time she goes live, I happen to be at work, or unavailable to join."

I'm surprised, and it shows in my stammering. "W-well, keep trying. She'll be happy you did. Won't you, Mimose?"

We hold our collective breath as Erzu responds with an elaborate twirl.

"Come on through," he says with admiration. "And good luck with that interview."

We're in!

CHAPTER TWELVE

Being *in* the parade at Carnival is a whole different ball game.

If people behind the barricades are spectators, all the major league players are in the street. You don't come out here unless you're ready and willing to stay active and march down the Parkway, dance with the crowd, and cheerlead for the float you're following. The people out here are usually younger and juiced up with energy.

Sometimes things can get rowdy—especially when there's mosh pit dancing going on. It's easy enough to avoid landing in one of those. All you have to do is pay attention to the music. We know the types of songs that will rile folks up. When that telltale beat drops that calls for elbows to jab and shoulders to shove, it's time to make your way to another float.

"Let's stick together," I tell Kwame and Renee, looping my arm through Erzu's.

Renee has got that shifty look again, like she's worried she'll see someone she knows. And Kwame is also on high alert, probably intent on avoiding his crew of "friends." I get it; they're more likely to be on this side of the barricade stirring up trouble that passes as fun in their book. And of course, my eyes get shifty every time I spy a pair of baggy jeans, because I'm still on the lookout for Juste.

But in this moment right here right now, I just want to soak it all in like Grandma Rose always told me to. She'd lean in close until I could smell hints of the lavender oil she used to soothe her muscle aches and she'd slowly say, "Just like there will never be another you—check the date, there will never be another today, especially exactly as it is now."

Funnily enough, Erzu seems to know this. I've never crossed paths with anyone more in the moment. I wish I could bottle up that whole vibe and share it with the world, because a lot of us could use a break from being shifty-eyed, or being on the run from judginess and shade.

I glance up at the clear sky. There's one type of shade that we would all welcome right now. No such luck. It's hard to tell how long it will take for the one white cloud to float its way over to cover the sun for a few seconds. I take my hair tie off my wrist and pull my hair up and off my neck in a ponytail. That's better.

The heat emanating from the frying-pan pavement must be scrambling my brain, because for the life of me, I can't place where I've seen the woman who's just walked up to me. She's wearing a tall headwrap and looks to be in her early twenties.

"Ohmygod, Baby Cicely! So good to see you," she says, her hand to her heart.

Before I can respond, Erzu jumps in and hugs the woman. She has a good-natured laugh and graciously accepts the hug. When the woman pats Erzu's back, I subtly try to count the number of rings she's wearing. There must be at least nine on each hand.

"Uh, that's my aunt Tati Mimose," I say, trying to cover up the awkward. "And these are my friends Renee and Kwame."

They both wave wordlessly. I want to glare at Renee and Kwame when neither of them take this opportunity to ask this woman her name. At least Erzu is making her feel like family. She's not even being super embarrassing about her fondness for this woman, which is nice.

But I'm having a hard time figuring out where I know this person from.

"Your grandmother was the best teacher I ever had," the woman tells me, and I am grateful for the context. "You were in grade school when she'd bring you to my art shows, but your face hasn't changed."

I immediately want to hug her. "I remember your art! As soon as I got home from seeing your work, I started cutting and pasting things all over the house."

She beams like my memory has been made real before her eyes. "And I bet your grandma made you feel like the next Bisa Butler," she laughs. Instead of asking the obvious questions, I make a mental note to look up Bisa Butler later. "Your grand-mother loved gushing about you. Matter of fact, you're looking a lot like her. Something about the way you carry yourself is exactly your grandma. I feel her presence here with you."

I look to my friends for their reaction to this private story, but they're in their own separate bubbles taking selfies with the scenery (Renee), photobombing those selfies (Erzu), or scanning the crowd like football stadium security (Kwame).

"I was actually just thinking of her," I fess up. Somehow this woman makes it easy to share this.

"Same!" She closes her eyes and smiles. "You know what popped into my head? The times she would tell us there's not another day like today. It's the way she would slow her words down to make sure they're all sinking in. That stays with me."

Hearing this gives my whole heart a sweet squeeze, but before I can respond, a group of the artist's friends appear, carrying sweating bottles of water.

"Hey, everybody," she tells her friends. "This is *the* Madame Benoirs's granddaughter, Cicely."

At the sound of my grandmother's name, the women all raise their water bottles. The girl with long braids even pours some water onto the pavement. "Let's pour some libation out for the leg-end," she says. "I will never forget her. I know she'd be proud of my next show coming up."

The cheers that go up in honor of Grandma Rose's memory catch all our attention, and they join the shouts when the libation girl sprinkles the rest of the water in the air. The droplets raining over us have a cooling effect, which feels great. We are washed, and I feel like we can go on a few more blocks in this heat.

Before we go our separate ways, the woman touches my arm. "Hey, I'll look you up on socials and DM you my info. If you ever need anything, or if you ever get serious about your cut-and-paste game, let me know."

I smile and politely nod at her. I can feel the seed of a thought take root in my mind. Up until now, I guess you could say I only dabbled in art. Hand-lettering, cutting and pasting images, quotes, fabric—it's just something I enjoyed doing for fun.

But could I get serious about my art?

I feel a little lighter for having met the woman whose name I guess I'll have to wait to find out if she DMs me.

"Did you wake up today thinking you'd have a street memorial for your grandma?" Kwame asks me as we walk on.

"Nothing about a day that has 'Meet Papash' on the calendar is turning out to be normal." I shake my head.

"I hear that."

Our pace comes to a halt when a woman in front of us backs up her bouncing bottom to the rhythm. We give her room because this clearly is her favorite song and we maybe would react the same way if it were ours. Her crochet bikini top is rocking her island flag colors and her blue-trimmed white shorts spell out BELIZE across her bottom.

If Erzu was letting loose before, now she's completely wildin' out. My aunt's neatly pulled-back braids are now free-flowing spiral tresses, and she does excited hair flips and shampoo commercial hair shakes.

"Yes, empress!" the woman in the Belize shorts calls out before the two of them dance together, back-to-back.

"Following the floats this year is buck wild." I duck away from flailing arms and gyrating hips. "More buck wild than I'd imagined."

"Not that you buy into it one hundred percent," shouts Renee. "But there's chatter online about this being a planetary alignment anomaly that's causing weirdness of mercury-in-retrograde proportions."

Renee checks her horoscope like she checks the forecast, though she'll swear it's just a habit. But considering Tati Mimose said something this morning about this event bringing peak spiritual energy, maybe a planetary alignment situation just compounds the whole effect the parade has on people. Could that explain why the possession happened to my aunt?

At least Erzu and her new friend are managing to proceed forward as they dance. We reach the Trinidadian float and marvel at their vibrant, feather-accented masquerade camp honoring the country's strong Native American heritage. I get mesmerized by the beaded feathers adorning their headdresses. Renee is beaming and in her element, greeting everyone in Trinidadian Creole and waving her flag as she goes. I'm thrilled for her and glad to see her loosen up.

The Haitian float is next. Seeing the ginormous Haitian flag on the truck gives me chills. Everyone out on Eastern Parkway are my people, but this right here is my family. The mob around the truck is spinning mostly Haitian and Jamaican flags in the air, and I spot a few folks wearing straw peasant hats, and even one person in that three-cornered hat of the eighteenth-century revolutionaries.

We all move clear of the body-slamming dance that accompanies their rara music. It is rampin'. But you have to be ready and willing to risk injury if you dive into that mosh pit for a good time. So we keep a bit of distance while cheering and dancing. I catch sight of the person with superhero arms on top of the speaker-stacked truck waving that giant red-and-blue Haitian drapo. The crowd goes wild for the high-pitched keyboard riff ringing out into the streets.

"You must feel good right about now," Kwame says, checking out my beaming face and bright smile.

"Something like that," I say with a grin.

We follow Renee and Erzu, all of us jumping up and dancing as we continue making our way past the float. Kwame is getting into it and waving his Pan-African flag in the air. His boys from J'Ouvert would wreak havoc with this float. I wonder if Kwame misses hanging with them at a time like this. I bump his shoulder in the same style as the Haitian rara dancers. He bumps mine back enthusiastically and I go hopping a few steps to the side.

"Whoa!" I warble.

"I'm so sorry!" Kwame grabs me apologetically with a sincere look on his face. "My bad. I didn't mean to."

"No, it's okay," I laugh. "You're fine. That's how the dance is done. But just don't think I won't get you back when you least expect it."

"I deserve that," he says with a nod.

"Okay, back to looking for butterflies," Renee says when we're past the Haitian float.

"Do you think the priestess's costume could be a representation of fairies instead of butterflies?" asks Kwame with sincere curiosity.

"You make it sound like butterflies get too much shine for a non-mystical creature."

His laugh makes it hard to look away from his face. "Nah, I'm just curious. Are island folks big on fairies or have I got that wrong?"

I purse my lips and process the question. "Hmm, I'm gonna guess that fairies aren't as big a thing as they may be in Europe? But then again, I think fairies in the islands may be known by another name. I'd have to look into that. But just take my word that it may score low in our mythology."

"You do know you don't speak for every last citizen on the islands," Kwame points out. "Especially being that you're here in Brooklyn, where you were born and raised."

"Sometimes you just know." I shrug. "Sometimes it's just a gut feeling. My island people can be pretty mystical, but we're a certain type of mystical."

"What do you mean by that?"

"Well, like take zombies. Zombies are totally our thing—you're welcome, Hollywood. But Dracula? Not so much. Though the islands do have bats. And Renee's told me about the soucouyant before, which has creepy bloodsucking tendencies," I explain.

I interrogate Renee every time she comes back from a trip to Trinidad. I've never been to Haiti, so any story she can share about island life, I eat it up.

Hearing her name, Renee turns and walks backward a few paces. "Ah yes, the soucouyant is a type of jumbie that drinks your blood at night and can shape-shift by day."

When Renee turns back around, Erzu locks arms with her, coaxing Renee to join her in her two-step dance.

"What else?" Kwame asks me.

"Yes to mermaids. No to Loch Ness Monster."

"Okay, that's obvious," says Kwame. "The Loch Ness would be our boy Scottish Scotty's vibe, not a Caribbean tradition. How about witches?"

"Now, the priestess is not a witch. Those are two different things. No shade to the witches, but I'd think a priestess tends to lean more toward God and spirituality."

"I see. All right, so maybe they're witches with rosary beads?"

"I like that," I laugh.

He nods. "How about werewolves? Yes to them?"

"You're getting it now. We rep for shape-shifters, werewolves, and zombies."

"Gotcha. Okay, I might circle back and ask more questions before the exam, if that's okay with you." Kwame knits his eyebrows and nods as if on official business.

"That's perfectly fine. Just check my office hours."

He looks at me and presses his lips together in a cute half smile.

I almost miss the Saint Kitts and Nevis float in all its purple-themed pageantry. Their beaded bikini costumes are figure-skater-fashion-meets-day-at-the-beach and the combo is explosive. As we make our way through, I dance extra hard to the soca music in honor of my namesake Cicely Tyson. I imagine her at the top of that float smiling down on Brooklyn.

"Here it comes!" Renee's shout tears into my thoughts.

I look to where she's pointing, and there, strutting in front of a truck draped in a banner advertising a local chiropractic practice, is who we've been searching for. Indeed, the costumed butterfly has wings that are so large it takes a wheeled contraption to support them.

"This has to be her," I say.

"That is so beautiful," breathes Renee in amazement.

Even Erzu is mesmerized. She's stopped dancing and starts staring at the shimmering effect that the wings are making against the sunlight. They must span over ten feet across, and yet the woman wearing the costume seems light on her feet and graceful, not at all weighed down by this huge winged contraption and feathered headdress. She looks elegantly comfy in a brown-skin-tone bodysuit accented with crystals.

"The butterfly chiropractor is mad young," says Kwame.

He's right. She looks about our age.

"She obviously can't be the chiropractor, but are we sure she's a priestess?" Renee asks.

"Only one way to find out," I say, making a move toward the float.

"Hey, Mimose, Mimose," comes a male voice from nearby.

I freeze. It can't be Juste, can it?

I turn to look. This guy, about Mimose's age, is dressed like he came straight from Wakanda, with an ornate neckpiece and muscular bare chest.

Kwame waves his hand in front of my face, and I realize that I haven't blinked in some time.

"Hi yourself," says a dazzled Renee.

The man greets us before turning to Mimose. "It's good to see you. It's been, what? Like, three years? I'm so glad that I ran into you. I went back to the building to see if I could get in touch with you, but you'd moved and I had no other way to find you."

"Oh my gosh, this is so romantic," says Renee.

"Are you not on social media?" I ask, wondering how he doesn't know about my aunt's celebrity.

He shakes his head. "Nah, it's not my thing."

Mimose comes up to him, puts her arms around him, and starts feeling on his chest.

"Oh, I guess you *have* thought of me, Mimose." He grins bashfully, caught off guard.

Oh no.

She runs her fingers along his jawline and squeezes his chin affectionately. Then she plays with his long locs and shimmies closer to him as she coos. She better not try to kiss him! I gasp, fully embarrassed.

"Oh, whoa, somebody's taking the 'spread love' message literally," jokes Renee.

"I can see that," the man says with a nod. "Uh, it's hard to talk here in the parade, so how about we connect when you're up for it? I can leave you my number if that works for you."

"We'll take that number," says Renee quickly.

He pulls out a card from I don't know where. Who knew that getup he's wearing has pockets, when the fashion industry can't find it in their patriarchal souls to put decent pockets in everyday women's wear.

"Here it is," he tells me. "If she forgets, you can remind her that Dresden would really love to reconnect with her," he says earnestly, handing his card over to us. I realize he thinks my aunt may be tipsy.

"Okay, that sounds good. We'll make sure to make that happen," Renee says.

"Please take care. If you need any help, feel free to call me. I can help you get her home, or whatever you have to do."

"Sure, sure. Thank you so much," Renee says hurriedly.

"That's really sweet of you," I say.

As he turns to walk away, Mimose runs over and hugs him from behind. She rests her head on the back of his shoulders with a happy grin.

"Whoa, okay, let's, let's dial it down a little bit," I say as we peel Erzu's arms off him. Renee mouths to me, *She's thirsty.* I nod, my eyes wide with disbelief. This is going to be pretty embarrassing when Mimose gets back in her body. Kwame can't stop chuckling.

Erzu pouts a little bit but seems satisfied.

"Erzu is no good for my aunt's love life," I say with a sigh once Dresden is out of earshot.

"She could set fire to it all in an afternoon if we're not careful," Renee says.

"We're going to miss the butterfly priestess," Kwame interjects, and he's right.

"The best way to do it is to act like part of the float," I say. "Come on, guys. You better get your dance on and represent best you can. Renee. Kwame. I hope you guys got that hip movement on lock. I want to see you wine."

At that moment, strangers join in to dance with us, nudging us behind the butterfly wing. The stained glass on the wings casts pretty colors on Kwame's face. Kwame holds out his hand for me. I take it and start to dance with him, but two girls suddenly have him sandwiched. I catch my smile melting and my jaw tensing a bit, which is ridiculous because I have no reason to be jealous. Let them have fun. This is Carnival. I turn to face another direction. And before long, a guy starts dancing behind me. It's time for my trick. I move my head to the side and smack the stranger with my ponytail.

"Hey, what was that about!"

I turn around and see it is Kwame.

"Oh my gosh, I'm so sorry. I thought you were another guy. I don't like dudes just pulling up on me," I say, embarrassed.

"You just left me there. So I had to come find you," Kwame explains.

"Well, you looked . . . busy."

"That doesn't sound jelly at all." Kwame smiles.

I shake my head. "You have the wrong impression. I want you to have fun. It's Carnival."

"Okay, but I think I'd have more fun dancing with you."

My heart thumps but I try not to react. So I squeal inwardly and match his corny little two-step. He spins me around. The butterfly wings swing back, casting the lights back toward us. Goofing around, we grab our phones and shoot our own music video with the fabulous lights.

"Ahem!" interrupts Renee, for good reason. I'm embarrassed I let myself lose focus when we're so close. The float has stopped moving, so now's the perfect time.

I hurry over to the teen priestess/possible chiropractor.

"Hello—er, Miss Butterfly," I greet her. "I know you're working and everything, but a friend sent us to ask you for your priestess services."

"Yes, we have a situation with a spirit," Renee adds.

"That needs to be evicted," jokes Kwame.

"Also, are you really a chiropractor who is also a priestess?" Renee asks.

Renee's journalism skills are unstoppable.

"Oh, wow. Okay, where do I start?" says Miss Butterfly. At least she doesn't sound annoyed. In fact, her strong air of confidence makes her sound much older than she looks. "To answer your question, my mom is the chiropractor, and yes, I'm a priestess. Do you have an issue trusting the expertise of teens who practice?"

"N-no, ma'am," I say, even though I'm sure we're around the same age.

I have so many follow-up questions for her. Like, why did I never consider that someone close to my age can be in a position to serve the community on this level? I open my mouth, but I stop myself, because that's a conversation for another day.

The priestess's face glitter catches the sun when she turns to me. "Now, my question to you is, which spirit are we talking about here?"

"Erzu—" I say, wishing I recalled the full, correct name.

"Erzulie? Sounds about right." She chuckles.

"Well, we kind of need this fast, so we're wondering how you can help us or if you have any advice so we can take care of it ourselves," I say, getting back to business.

"I can give you advice, but you would need these hands to perform it."

"But you're busy," Renee remarks.

"I guess you can say that, yes," she says while waving her wings. "What I can do for you is this: If you bring her to me now, I can say a few prayers to see if the spirit can be expelled. Do you have the materials I need?"

We look at one another, no doubt thinking about the missing rosary beads. "Mostly," I say.

"Okay, then. By the next corner. I'll be looking out for you."

"Thank you so much," I say.

We turn to one another for a quick huddle.

"Let's put this plan in action." I peek inside Renee's tote bag. "Are we ready with supplies? Check." I answer my own question. Next, I look to Kwame. "Kwame, are you ready to make a hole through the crowd so that we can beat the priestess to the next stop?"

"Check."

"Renee, do you have Erzu?"

Renee looks down at the hand she is holding. The color drains from her face when she doesn't recognize the woman it's attached to.

"No. She's gone!"

CHAPTER THIRTEEN

"Okay, we have to stay calm and realize that there's got to be a solution to this," says Kwame.

"*Okay,*" I snap, panicking. "The solution being that we need help."

"I think that guy has Tati Mimose," Renee blurts.

"That guy, the guy that was here?" I say, glancing around. "The guy Dresden?"

"Yes, if that's his name," Renee puffs. "It was really weird for him to just come out of nowhere and recognize her and have all this backstory. And she'd not be able to corroborate that. Don't you think that's a little sus?"

I hadn't been suspicious of the guy at the time, but I see what Renee is saying. I glance around frantically. Where is my aunt?

"Hey, Dresden and Juste could be one and the same," adds Kwame, before miming that his mind is exploding.

"There's clearly a night-and-day difference between them."
I pat his shoulder like, *Nice try.*

Kwame points at me. "Didn't you just say something about shape-shifters earlier?"

I pivot on one foot and walk backward, smiling at him. "Oh, I see you're trying to be an honorary Caribbean, understanding that the real and the magic can coexist."

He walks forward, grinning mischievously and matching my steps. "Well, you know, I'm not passing judgment."

Renee claps several times, breaking our spell. "Dresden hasn't been gone long. Maybe we can find him. He's tall enough to stand out in the crowd."

"Okay, that's a plan." I quick-spin and march forward.

Kwame turns to me. "Let me give you a boost so you can look over the crowd and spot him."

"A shoulder boost? It's been a minute since I've done that."

"I'll spot you and make sure you don't topple," Renee says.

"Okay, fine."

Kwame bends over and offers up his interlaced fingers for my foot.

"Wait," I say. "I've been stepping in goodness-knows-what all day today."

"Yuck, good point." Kwame takes his hands away. "Just check your sneakers and it'll be okay."

When I kick back my feet to inspect the soles, Renee and I see something unidentifiable under there.

"Go and wipe them on something," she suggests.

"On what?"

"Find some grass."

Kwame looks incredulous. "In the middle of Eastern Parkway?"

"Here, I have a napkin I got from my parents' stand." I take the napkin from my pocket and place it in Kwame's cupped hands for the padding he needs to keep his palms clean.

But then I just stare at the napkin. There's no smooth way to do this. I'll be essentially climbing my crush like a ladder. I know we've been in tight spaces together all morning, but I've never had to climb him. That's next-level up close. Am I even sure I don't smell sweaty? We've done a lot of walking.

The longer I take to make that move, the harder it is to just do it.

Finally, I take a deep breath and step into Kwame's interlaced hands. Once I'm off the ground, I press down on his sturdy shoulders—*focus, Cicely!*—and hoist myself up. As soon as I get enough height, I pivot, swinging my free leg over his shoulder. And I do it all with jelly-weak knees that will only function normally when I'm not this close to Kwame.

Kwame is the first to break the awkward silence. "Uh, s-see anything yet?"

Oh, that's right. I'm up here to scout. I swallow and focus on the middle distance. And then I sigh regretfully. "I should've worn my glasses today."

"Are you kidding me?" shrieks Renee. "This is the worst."

I squint and frown at the same time. "I don't know what we're gonna do if we don't find her."

Renee looks apologetic. "I was talking about my phone's low-battery alert."

"Oh, that is bad," I say sympathetically, because I know what a lifeline Renee's phone is to her.

Still, she sympathizes with me. "Don't worry, you got this."

"Yeah, you can shut your phone off for an hour, and we'll cover you in the meantime," I say while scanning the crowd. Then—

"I see him!" I shout in all confidence. But I follow up with "I think I see him. He's one block up, buying something from a vendor."

Renee gasps.

"Keep your eye on him," instructs Kwame, walking forward.

"Yo, you're moving too fast. I feel like I'm gonna fall over," I panic. "I'm too tall for this. You can't walk with me." I get nervous and steady myself by clutching Kwame's head.

"Well, I can't walk if you block my eyes," grunts Kwame. "Can you please move your hands? I can't see where I'm going."

"Okay, y'all are becoming a sideshow and this is serious business," warns Renee.

"Okay, get down," Kwame breathes.

I pretend to kiss the ground after Kwame helps me down—rather gallantly, I might add. Recovered, I lead Renee and Kwame to where I spotted Dresden.

We walk as fast as one can when making our way through costumed dancers dressed as Afrofuturist graphic novel characters come to life.

We have a visual of the water vendor now, and there's a group of people around the stand. But Dresden is not one of them. Neither is my aunt.

"Look over there," shouts Renee.

There is a tall person standing head and shoulders above the crowd.

"Dresden," I confirm.

He has his muscular brown arm slung around a woman's shoulder. It's hard to make out who the woman is, but we're pretty sure it's Mimose; she's the same height. But the crowds don't let me see my aunt clearly.

"I'm going in," I say. I zigzag around people and make my way over there. My friends try to keep up.

"Yo!" somebody shouts at us as we zip through like a ball ricocheting around a pinball machine.

"Quit pushing!" someone else shouts.

"Sorry!" Kwame yells back.

Soon I'm tapping on Dresden's solid arm.

"Let go of her, you kidnapper. How dare you take her?" I growl.

"Knowing the state she's in," Renee adds. She's right behind me, panting but ready.

Dresden turns around, confusion etched in his eyebrows.

"What are you talking about?" he asks. It's then that we see that it's an older woman at his side. "This is my mom."

"Dresden, what's going on?" his mother asks.

"Nothing, Mummy, I'm just going to assume this is a unique circumstance and these kids are not usually this disrespectful."

"I'm—we're . . . so sorry," I offer in all sincerity. "Excuse us. We're just gonna go now."

We turn to leave, but Dresden won't let us off the hook that easily.

"Wait. You lost her? And you thought that, what? Maybe I took advantage and took her away?" he fumes.

"Well, we didn't know what to think," Renee says.

"Yeah, you could've been a shape-shifter," adds Kwame.

Dresden blinks a couple of times before shaking his head. "I'm not going to say more because I see you're clearly worried. Where are your parents?"

"My mom is working at her vendor station. Here's a flyer," I say, and hand him a Port-au-Princesse flyer out of desperation. He takes it out of kindness.

"Why don't you check there?" he asks.

"Yes. Okay."

We walk away shamefaced, but not in the direction of my mom's stand. We're not that desperate yet.

"So what do we do?" asks Kwame.

"Let's text Jovita," Renee suggests. "Maybe she has some sort of a GPS tracker for Mimose's phone."

"It's worth a try," I say.

I text Jovita the SOS and she immediately responds that she doesn't track her boss's phone. And she's still tracking down the rosary beads.

"What now?" I ask Renee and Kwame. I check my phone. "The podcast is going to start in, like, ten minutes."

Go see your mom.

The voice pops into my head before I can stop it. Grandma Rose would say that's my intuition talking, and the intuition should be respected for its wisdom.

"Why don't we go back to your mom and ask if she's seen Mimose?" says Renee.

Sign number two. Yet something stubborn in me won't yield to this advice.

"Isn't there a booth where they make announcements for lost toddlers here?" I ask in a last attempt. I'd rather avoid involving my mom if I can help it. What would I even tell her? I met up with Mimose today and she got me involved in Vodou again?

"I don't think so," Renee says softly.

I can't believe that it's come to this. My eyes start to blur but I blink back the tears. I give one last frantic look around me until I feel a comforting touch on my upper back. It sends a calm through me. Kwame is standing next to me, and his hand lightly rests there. Our eyes meet but he doesn't say a word. His presence and steadiness are his silent offer.

I take a deep breath, look at my friends, and say calmly, "You're right. I guess it is time we go to my mom."

"What are you going to tell her?" asks Renee, who's been staying very close by me like I'm her new charge.

"I don't know. I think I'll have to tell her the truth."

"Maybe she knows where her sister could have gone?"

"I don't—I don't know. There's only one way to find out."

We see a good number of people lined up at the booth for my mom's food, which is a happy surprise. Kwame and Renee stay a distance away as I walk behind the booth to talk to Mom.

As soon as I see her, no part of me wants to trip up her cheerful working rhythm. She looks like she's enjoying herself, and if there's a subject that will kill my mom's mood in no time flat, it's her kid sister. But the sight of my comforting mother also makes me want to upchuck every detail about the whole day. That part of me just might win this battle.

"Oh, Cicely, you're back!" Mom greets me before I have a chance to choose either way. "Your flyers have been working. That was a great idea, sweetie."

"Great, I'm glad," I say, my vocal cords quivering like they're being personally strummed by The Anxiety. And then as nonchalantly as possible, "Have you run into Tati Mimose today?"

"She came over here talking some nonsense I couldn't even

understand. And I have no bandwidth to understand. She was acting kooky, if you asked me. I can't deal with her right now."

"Do you know where she went?"

Mom shakes her head.

"What do you think she wanted?"

"I didn't pay much attention to her. There was a customer complaint I was dealing with at the time."

"So what happened?" I ask, my heart racing even as I keep trying to act like everything is normal.

"Oh, somebody claimed that they asked for griot, not fish."

"No, no, what happened to Tati Mimose after that?"

"I don't know. She was here and then she wasn't. I told her to hold on and I'd talk with her, but she bounced. Your dad ran back to get more supplies out the van, and so I was short one person. Hey, honey." Mom frowns at me. "You good?"

I smile and nod, choosing to remain silent because I'm liable to say more than I'm prepared to right now.

"Keep handing out those flyers. They're helping. We had to re-up!"

"Cool" is all I manage to say.

"And these are for you and your friends," Mom says, handing me three cold bottles of fruit-flavored island sodas.

"Thanks, Mom," I say. I pause, wishing I could spend more time helping her. Instead of being at her side serving up fish fry, I've got bigger fish to fry.

With the soda bottles in hand, I'm realizing how

thirsty—and hungry—I am. I buy some Jamaican beef patties at the booth next to my parents' and carry everything over to Renee and Kwame. We devour the patties and gulp down the sodas while nursing our ache over having no leads on my aunt's whereabouts.

"I think we have to go to the podcast stage." I sigh and press my fingers to both of my temples. "And tell them that we can't find Mimose."

Renee nods. "I hate to admit it, but yeah."

Even the idea that I might see Papash there doesn't bring me much joy.

I have to face facts, because we're all out of options.

CHAPTER FOURTEEN

Jovita texts us directions to the podcast stage, and within five minutes, we're at the fenced-in parking lot adjacent to a mini-mart. There's a raised platform set up in front of the colorful mural depicting all the island fruits and veggies on offer in the mini-mart. Floating plantains, breadfruit, mango, ackee, and leafy callaloo make the perfect backdrop. Cameras are pointed at the stage and the huge white banner overhead reads: THE "GOODCHAT PRESENTS" SERIES. I know nothing about audio equipment, but the mics set up on the stage look top grade.

All the revelry and music from nearby Eastern Parkway are close enough to hear but distant enough to provide the perfect ambient sound to give any podcast listener that atmospheric vibe.

A cop standing at the parking lot entrance is busy giving directions to a production crew carrying some type of big furry speaker. Maybe they're heading out to record all those person-on-the-street soundbites you sometimes hear during podcast episodes.

"C'mon, y'all," Kwame says low enough for our ears only. "Now's our chance to walk in."

Confused, I look at him. "But the guard is busy."

"That's the whole point," answers Renee.

Kwame slips in first, and we're right behind him. I've never done anything like this, and it shows. I walk through like I'm silently freaked out about a spider on my shoulder.

No sign of my aunt, or Papash. Now that we're closer to the stage, I see it's on wheels, but secured by cinder blocks placed on either side of the jumbo tires. It makes me imagine how amazing it would be if my aunt were invited to ride through the parade with Papash.

We go up to the pacing woman wearing a headset over her crudely styled ponytail.

"You shouldn't be here," says the woman. She extends her pacing over to the three of us. "This is a special event. You're gonna have to leave."

"Um," I say nervously. "My aunt is Mimose Benoirs, and—"

"Oh my goodness, Jovita? I'm so glad that you're here!" the woman exclaims, looking relieved. "I called your cell but got no answer."

I open my mouth but glance at my friends before I put any words together. "Yeah, about that, uh—"

"Mimose had been approved for a plus-two, not a plus-three."

The woman gives Renee and Kwame a quick once-over. "But anyway, I was trying to get the message to you that the podcast taping is as of now on hold because of . . . unforeseen delays."

I mentally play back the last thing she said. "By on hold, you mean . . ." We lean in to hear an answer that's not coming.

I ask in a more direct way. "Do you have a new time when Mimose should get here?"

The woman looks around as if to see if the coast is clear. And then she reaches into her back pocket and twists the knob on the microphone base unit clipped there.

"Quite frankly, no," she admits. "Between you and me, there's talk of postponing the interview to a later date."

"Oh no!" says Renee. "That's a shame."

I'm relieved that Mimose isn't late for her interview. But why do they want to postpone it?

"Are they just going to end up canceling the whole thing?" I ask, worried.

The woman shakes her head. "Oh, honey, not when they've lined up big sponsors for this interview. I thought Carnival was big when a few mas camp designs ended up at Paris Fashion Week. But voodoo is trending even bigger now. Hollywood is set to release a voodoo thriller with A-list stars, and we've got its streamer to sponsor this interview. I let Mimose know all about it."

My friends and I turn to one another as the woman answers a communication on her headset. I suddenly feel skeeved out.

Would my aunt really be okay with selling Vodou in this way?

"That doesn't sound like something Mimose would approve of," says Renee.

"Maybe your aunt knows and doesn't mind," suggests Kwame.

"Or maybe she does, and she's just looking for more clout? I mean, it is tempting. Being on a podcast with Papash gets her name out there in a big way," I say.

We barely have enough time to take in what we've just heard when we catch sight of him. Not Papash, but an overgrown frat-guy-turned-exec in a suit. He marches up to the woman, lanyard swinging, face scrunched up in fury, fists balled up.

"Where is Papash?" he growls.

The woman is taken aback. "He's, uh—he's running late . . ."

"You mean you lost him? How is that even possible?"

The woman, whom I'm assuming is the producer, looks like she wants to let loose on the executive, but she bites her tongue. "I knew booking a musician would be a risk."

"And where's the influencer?" the suit guy demands.

The producer gestures at me. "This is Mimose's intern."

"Hi—hi," I stammer. "Mimose, is, um, busy right now."

The guy turns to me. Suddenly, I'm no longer invisible to him, and he's all smiles.

"Apparently your Mimose is turning herself into quite the brand," he says. "I just saw a photo of her—she totally has a face for TV. And people are really digging that spiritualism thing.

That whole aesthetic can work for us if we present it right. We can take voodoo mainstream."

I don't even know how to respond to that. *Does* my aunt know that the people handling her interview feel this way?

"Let's go, y'all," I tell Renee and Kwame. We've clearly heard enough.

"Wait, I'd like your help with something," the exec calls. I glance back. "I'd like Mimose to call Papash and ask him to report to our soundstage ASAP. There's something in it for her. Even if she doesn't get her podcast taping today, we can postpone it to a day that suits her."

Renee and I eye each other but don't say a word.

"Our producer can give you Papash's direct number," the suit guys adds, nodding to the ponytail woman. "Are we agreed?"

Papash's number? A direct line to THE Papash? How can we say no?

I nod slowly, and Kwame lets out what sounds like all the air his cheeks could store.

Renee is definitely in my corner, because she takes my arm and practically pulls me back to the producer to get that contact information.

"Jovita, yes?" the producer asks.

"Jovita," I state rather than confirm.

"Good. This number is confidential, so please do not share it with anyone."

"Jovita," I state again.

The producer gives me a quizzical stare, and I stay super still in the hopes that she forgets what's just happened. It works. She continues laying down a few ground rules and then reads me Papash's number. I enter it into my phone, and then Renee, Kwame, and I head off.

"This is so wild," says Kwame says once we're out of earshot.

"Where do you think Papash could be?" I wonder.

"Could be he just overslept or something," guesses Renee. "Maybe he was up all night at J'Ouvert."

"Maybe so," I say in a small voice.

"Only one way to find out," Kwame says.

I pull my phone out my back pocket and touch the galaxy case as if for the first time. Papash's number is in this phone. *Papash's direct line.*

"Uh, you okay there?" Kwame watches me closely.

"Um, yeah," I chuckle. "It's just not every day I get handed Papash's number."

Only on Caribbean Christmas.

"Well, one thing's for sure," Renee says. "We can't call him until we find your aunt. She's the one he wants to speak to. It'll have to be up to her."

We're not too far from Kwame's building, so we decide to head there to regroup. Renee can charge her phone, and we can take a minute to strategize. As long as Juste isn't there, we'll be okay. I hope.

CHAPTER FIFTEEN

Kwame plants a foot on the stone steps of his building like it's the peak of Mount Everest. "All roads lead home," he proclaims.

Kofi meets us on the front stoop. "Welcome, welcome!"

"We're back where this all started," says Renee, her hand shielding her eyes from the sun as she gazes up Kwame's urban mountain, the four-story prewar building that really does have one of the best views of the parade.

I think back a few hours to the moment when the sight of the brick-face structure with the ornate stonework gave me the flutters. That was before I knew that the place that housed someone like Kwame also harbored someone like Juste. But anyone who's ever thought hateful thoughts so foreign to their own heart knows that good and evil can lie under one roof. If the lesson here is where there's good, there's bad, I'd rather think of it in the reverse. Where's there's bad, there's also good.

"I'll go charge your phone," Kofi tells Renee. "You need anything?"

"I've been holding it for a while. Can I use your bathroom?" Renee asks, following him inside.

"Let me go see what that ice cream truck is saying." Kwame pulls a few crumpled bills from his front pocket and takes a couple of paces toward the people lined up before a parked vendor. He suddenly halts, turns on his heel, and walks back over to me. "Cicely?"

I blink away my swirling thoughts and meet his eyes. My breath catches on the earnestness I discover there.

I keep my voice as casual and chill as possible. "What's up?"

After an intake of breath, Kwame lets a string of words tumble lightly from his mouth. "Can I take you out for ice cream?"

Suddenly, I hate reflexes. In my opinion, reflexes should only serve to reduce harm. The fact that the giddy smile reflexively spreading across my face makes me so vulnerable to rejection is textbook harmful. Reflexes should stick to yanking fingers from a hot stove or pushing unsuspecting pedestrians out the path of runaway buses.

Now, thanks to my face, there's little mystery about how I feel for the boy standing before me.

But that smile seems like just the signal Kwame is hoping for. He boyishly returns it. Next, he holds out his arm, which I take. Together, we stroll over to the back of the dessert truck's line.

This day has been so wacky, I feel prepared to expect any- and everything. But this sweet and simple moment is one scenario I feel happily surprised by. We've only walked a few paces to this line, yet it feels like a time-out from our search for Mimose, from our all-day stressing.

For the first time since this morning, I feel as normal as all the people around me. They are here to just chill and enjoy, meet up and hang out, celebrate and party. And right now, Kwame and I are simply enjoying each other's company—and that feels like a luxury I'm super grateful for.

I think back to how embarrassed I felt knowing Kwame would have a front-row seat to this whole day. I was always taught to handle family issues in private. Plus, there was a very real possibility Kwame would judge me, and worse—blab to everyone at school about what had gone down. I didn't imagine all the good things he would add to this day.

"So, how are you?" Kwame asks.

And I smile, because he's not making small talk for any reason other than to . . . talk to me.

"I'm having a good time . . . right this second."

He pretends to be disappointed. "Well, I need to work harder to keep that feeling lasting longer than a second."

My head is buzzing. And so is my phone. It's a text from Jovita.

"Jovita's got the rosary," I paraphrase her message. "She ended up getting the prayer beads from my aunt's house, of all places. But my aunt wasn't there." I text Jovita where we are now, then step forward to order our ice cream cones.

Moments later, Kwame and I lean against a nearby brick

wall with our treats: a vanilla cone for me, and an ice pop for Kwame. Renee and Kofi have come back outside and are in line to order at the truck, too. Renee's phone has more of a charge now, and she's showing Kofi her account, no doubt loving that she's got an intern she can show the reporting ropes to.

I know that to someone like Renee, everything that's happened so far today is the ultimate newsworthy story. But thankfully, she has tamped down her impulses and hasn't put anything on social media. She probably has a ton of questions, and I love her for not asking them all.

Right now, all I can think about is what I learned at the podcast stage, and what my aunt did—and didn't—know about the people behind the podcast. When Kwame glances at me and asks me what's wrong, I tell him just that.

"You know," says Kwame, rubbing his ice pop wrapper between his hands and looking into the distance at all the confetti of color and movement. "Whether or not your aunt knew about the sponsors for her interview, I've learned that sometimes people don't make the choice you expect them to make. But that doesn't make their hearts less sincere."

I don't say anything. I focus on my ice cream cone.

"Sometimes it's just that they're not up for the type of courage it takes to change course. Sometimes they're too far in and don't know their way out," he continues.

"Are you speaking from personal experience?" I ask with a splash of attitude.

His eyebrows knit together. "What's that supposed to mean?"

"I don't know, just that I've noticed that you act one way in private and another in public."

He shrugs. "Don't we all?"

"Yes, I guess. But I always thought my aunt was more authentic than that. She's somebody people easily follow. Not someone who is begging for followers."

"Yeah. But have you noticed, if she wants those people to follow her, there's certain things she's got to do? People are not going to follow unless they get something out of it."

"What about wisdom and good advice?"

It's like Kwame believes adopting an apologetic expression makes his point land more softly. "They can get that from their grandma on Sunday morning."

The mention of grandmothers instantly makes me forget my rebuttal. Kwame gently fills the silence.

"We all just really want to be accepted. Even somebody like your aunt," he says. "Just because she's popular or cool doesn't mean she doesn't want to be accepted."

Since when is Kwame an expert on *my* aunt? My aunt whom I've known and admired my entire life. My aunt who has literally taught me what courage and authenticity is every step of the way. I keep my annoyance at bay and say evenly, "Listen, I know that's a universal feeling, but I don't think she's here for that. She's here to help people understand themselves better."

"That's a lot of pressure to be all things to all people,"

Kwame says. "And that's not to say everything you tell me about your aunt isn't true. I'm just saying you're looking at her like she's changed, or she's not the person you think she was, just off of this one deal."

"Well, it happens to be a very big deal. It stands against her core principles and beliefs."

I catch sight of the back of a Philippines flag T-shirt worn by a person in the ice cream truck crowd. I do a double take because the shirt-wearing person is the same height and build as Sister Lucille. It would be wild if she abandoned her nun attire for a day to come out here. Would we even recognize her if she did?

Kwame walks across the sidewalk to the bin and tosses the wrapper in the trash. When he returns, he faces me. "Oh yeah, what does your aunt believe in?"

Having lost sight of the Sister Lucille lookalike, I answer, "She believes in lifting up people. Helping people find their personal power beyond what they can see with their eyes."

"So what's changed?"

"What's changed is she may choose to team up with those podcast people. And if so, she'd be a huckster, selling out her culture, just to make a buck."

It looks like I finally hit a nerve. Kwame's face bunches up like he's confused and his voice is a little strained. "People just love tossing around that 'selling out' phrase. I don't have an opinion on whether or not she sold out. I'm just saying we should take a step back if you really want to talk to her and get answers. She's not gonna want to talk if your mind's already made up. She's gonna feel that."

"You sound like a Tati Mimose expert," I sniff.

Kwame shrugs his shoulders. "I'm just sayin'."

He's just sayin'? Nobody uses that phrase unless they've just said something out of pocket. I'm stewing on this so hard, I totally miss the echoes of excited commotion coming down Eastern Parkway.

I can tell Kwame catches the forlorn look on my face, because his voice has softened again. "Look, all I'm saying is we shouldn't be quick to judgment."

I snap. "How am I judging? I just needed some time to let this sink in. I'm kind of hurt by what's happening. My aunt is lost. I got you all involved in this. And this is supposed to be one of my happiest days of the year."

"I get it. I'm sorry for everything that's happened. I'm just . . . just trying to help."

More like trying to make me feel guilty. "So, all right, you know what, I'm grateful for all your help today," I say sharply. "But that doesn't mean I'll let you stomp into my family business. There's a lot you don't know and I'd really appreciate it if you don't act like you do. If we're being real about this, I have some quick takes on your family that may not be easy for *you* to hear."

"Whoa, whoa, what's going on?" comes Sekou's distinct voice.

We were so involved in our disagreement, we didn't notice Kwame's big brother walking up the street. "Trouble in paradise? I bet I can hear you guys from our place."

I doubt that, considering how loud their AC unit is.

Kwame's chest falls, and I swear he looks an inch shorter. "Nothing you need to worry about," he tells Sekou.

"Well, I did warn you, little bro. Birds of a feather, and all that. You start hanging with it, start acting like it—taking dramas to the streets and whatnot."

"Sekou, serious question," I begin, unable to tolerate his smug attitude anymore. "What do you have against your brother? You can't stop harping on him, and I want to know why."

Kwame tries to appeal to me. "Cicely, we should get going. It's not worth talking about this."

Sekou's bellow is full of amusement. "No, this is good. We're getting stuff out and clearing the air. I think your question should be, what does Kwame have against his brothers? Namely, Kofi."

I'm really confused, and my face shows it. Kwame is far from cruel to his kid brother. "Now you're reaching," I say with a flip of my twisty ponytail.

"My brother knows what I'm talking about," Sekou answers breezily, like he's not actively trying to assassinate Kwame's character. He even cracks a smile when he looks at his brother. "You didn't tell her about your whole freshman-year act that threw you off of being an honors student last year. Oh, no? Well, ole boy here missed out on a scholarship because he didn't *want* to be an honors student last year. He wanted to have the knucklehead freshman experience with his friends, so he screwed up the entrance exam on purpose."

I throw a glance at Renee and Kofi, and they seem unaware of this unbrotherly clash going on a few yards from them. Renee looks like she's still in intern tutorial mode as they eat their ice cream bars.

"Back off, yo." Kwame's warning is sadly as effective as it was when he used it against Juste.

"You didn't think it would cost you a scholarship," Sekou goes on. "You didn't think our parents having to come a hundred percent out of pocket would mess with the money they'd saved for Kofi's tuition."

"That's not exactly how it happened," refutes Kwame.

"Well, Kofi will make do next year at some school around the way. And, hey, it's awesome you're able to catch up now, even though your *friends* tease you about selling out. That reminds me—the other day on the ball court, I hardly recognized you. Must be exhausting jumping through hoops like that—pun intended—just to get them to like you."

"I don't have to listen to his." Kwame pushes himself off the wall and turns to me. "Cicely. If you need anything, call me."

And with that, he storms into his building. Back to the low-key Labor Day he had been planning on until I showed up at his door this morning.

The ice cream barely cooled me down on this hot day, but Kwame's absence leaves a slight chill in the air.

"Yo, where're you going?" Kofi yells after Kwame, but Kwame doesn't answer.

I heave out a sigh. What is it with siblings tearing down their relationships? I would give anything for a sibling, yet everywhere I look it's brother versus brother, sister versus sister . . .

Sekou stands, arms crossed. His face sags with the weight of his guilt. That's not going to save him from hearing my piece.

"Your work is done here," I tell Sekou. "You got rid of him. You can move on."

Too stubborn to own up to things and too pompous to see he's become the street drama he poked fun at moments ago, he answers, "He was gonna ditch y'all for his fake friends sooner or later."

"So you want to turn everybody away from him, is that it? You act like you've never made a mistake in your life. How long is he gonna have to pay for this?"

I'm reminded of how Kwame just told me that I was being too hard on my aunt. But this is different. Mimose is a whole adult. What's the use of being a teen if people don't let you outgrow your mistakes and move past them? Sekou is like a living ghost, actively haunting his brother, holding him up and clanging reminders of misdeeds like chains.

Sekou doesn't respond, but he looks thoughtful. I wonder if I got through to him.

"Cicely, you see that?" Renee barely gets the words out before she lets loose a deep-voiced shriek. She's goes berserk jumping up and down and waving her Trini flag in the air at the shiny chrome-plated truck passing by.

I look over and my mouth drops open. There is Papash, standing on top of jumbo speakers like the conqueror of music that he is. The speakers under him are silent at the moment. But he doesn't need to drop a beat or utter a word into his mic for me to identify him. I'd know that outstretched-arm stance anywhere. It's as recognizable to me as the ball-dunking Jordan silhouette. This is Papash in all his Brooklyn-embracing glory.

"Ohmygod, it's Papash!" I scream at Renee like I'm the one breaking the news to her. "It's Papash!"

So that's where he's been!

As "Sensational" blasts from the speakers and Papash begins singing on his one-man float, the crowds on the sidewalk cheer. People rush into the street, trying to join the float or record the best video. Heads poke out of building windows and people hop out onto their fire escapes. Papash's performance might as well be a flame-throwing act, because everything and everyone is lit.

Renee throws her head back and laughs at Papash's mischievous genius. She throws her hands in the air. "He's doing this for the culture, y'all! So heck yeah, the media and the interviews can wait. The people come first!"

I'm so stunned by what I'm seeing that I don't join in with

the dancing. I stand there, mesmerized. This is the biggest thrill, and yet the most worried I've felt all day.

I scan the throng of dancers following the float for a sign of my aunt. But she's not there. I would've thought that somehow, Papash's performance would have drawn her out of hiding.

Then I feel a familiar hand on my arm. I look behind me and see that Papash's performance has brought one person back: Kwame. He gives me a small smile, and together we watch Papash's float make its triumphant way down the street.

CHAPTER SIXTEEN

Moments after Papash has gone, Renee runs over to me with another news flash.

"We've got a Mimose sighting not far from here!" she calls, holding up her phone.

"What do you mean?" I ask.

"I was scrolling through Instagram posts, and everyone's sharing videos from the parade," Renee explains while Kofi nods excitedly beside her. "And look—she's on the Nutriment float."

Renee holds up her screen to show my aunt dancing under a cloud of talcum powder. She looks like she's having the time of her life. My heart skips with happy relief.

"Wait, how many minutes ago was this?" asks Sekou, suddenly serious and realizing our plight. Before we can ask how he knows what's going on, he explains, "Kofi caught me up."

I nod, grateful for Kofi.

"This was posted two minutes ago," Renee answers.

Kwame reaches for Renee's phone. "Let me take a closer look."

I lean in as he zooms into the street sign in the background.

"Franklin Avenue," I confirm. "We could get there in like five minutes if we run."

"Well, then we need to move quick," Renee says.

Renee, Kofi, Kwame, and I take all but two steps and bump right into someone.

It's Jovita with the rosary beads.

"I wish I could stay longer, but I'm juggling a few things today—er, not other clients," she says hurriedly.

"It's okay," I tell her, gratefully accepting the beads. I hand them over to Renee, who stashes them in her tote bag. "We actually have to run, too. Thanks so much for all your help today."

She nods. "Text me if you need me. I'll be at the *Today* show soundstage where the masquerade fashion show is happening," she says. "I . . . heard."

I give Jovita a wink—the fact that she has other clients besides my aunt is safe with me. Renee, Kwame, Kofi, Sekou, and I turn and head out in the opposite direction, but we hit a wall of more people.

"How are we gonna run through this crowd?" Kofi shouts.

"Follow me," Sekou says.

He trots back toward his building and I feel my annoyance rising. "This is the opposite direction."

Sekou is now on his phone, talking to a friend of his who's sticking his head outside the Hilliard family window. We see a thumbs-up signal out the window before two Mary Poppins–looking umbrellas are tossed to the small green patch of grass outside the building.

Kofi beams as Sekou goes to collect the umbrellas.

"What's going on?" I ask.

Kofi explains, "Sekou got inspired by the low-tech genius of Hong Kong protests. He devised this for himself and Kwame to get supplies and help Black Lives Matter crowds during the uprising. Don't worry, the umbrellas are poke-free, thanks to soft protectors on the spokes of the umbrellas."

"Kwame, let's do this!" Sekou yells, handing one umbrella to his brother. They lock arms with each other. When they open the large, spoke-protected umbrellas and point them at a ninety-degree angle, we take their cue and join them—me standing behind Kwame and Renee behind Sekou, with Kofi between us—like they're conductors of the Eastern Parkway express train.

It works! With their umbrellas, Kwame and Sekou carve a tunnel through the throngs until we are able to keep a nice jogging pace. Kwame and Sekou keep their arms linked and I even hear them chuckling a few times. It's hard not to grin, too. This is actually fun, and the parade-goers seem to respect it.

"Aaaaye, it's the Um-bro-las!" comes a shout from the crowd, and I can't believe a few people remember Kwame and Sekou from the uprisings.

I'm amazed what siblings can accomplish when they work together. This is what I want for my mom and aunt.

"Avoid the northwest corner of the street," Renee calls out as she checks her phone. "There's a barricade there."

"Got it," Kwame answers.

And suddenly, we arrive at where the Nutriment float is. We see the powdery cloud before we can make out any people.

Just when the air clears, a ghostly cloud swallows us again. Someone goes around tossing more powder. What's the significance of this, anyway?

I do absolutely the wrong thing and look up. Talcum gets in my eye.

"Oh my gosh," I whine. "It's in my eye. Is this gonna cause cancer later or something?"

"I have some water," Kwame says, being his usual helpful self. He's holding the water bottle to my face, ready to pour a bit when I'm ready. And I feel terrible about how harsh I was to him.

"I don't want to use all your water," I say. He looks at my hand that I've placed gently over his water bottle.

"But this is an emergency," he argues. "Let me help."

My clownery for looking up when powder is raining down is much different than the tear-gassed eyes Kwame got used to cleaning out when he was marching at protests.

"I'm sorry for earlier," I tell him, even if I can't see him clearly at the moment. My sensitive eyes are crying out for water.

Kwame lightly touches my cheek with his other hand and says softly, "It's fine. Now, let me help you get that under control."

As Kwame pours the water out, I can't help but concentrate on the pads of his fingers on my face. The water sometimes misses its target, but it does the job. My eyes are free of the talcum powder now.

"I'm sorry," he says. "Some of it got into your hair."

"That's all right." I shrug. "My hair loves water. It could use the moisture anyway."

"I just always thought—" He pauses, and then his eyes sweep over my face like he wants to touch it again. "Oh, okay."

I clear my throat, even though it's the flutters in my chest that need clearing. "Thanks for that, Kwame. I feel better now. You?"

He smiles, and I'm glad I'm able to clearly see it. "I do, too."

I look back at the float, and now Tati Mimose is easy to pick out. She's the sun around which everyone revolves. And she is partying like she doesn't have anywhere else to be.

My smile fades. While my mother is working her butt off on one end of Eastern Parkway, look what my aunt is doing on the other. This must be what my mother meant all those years ago. *Look at how she chooses to use her influence.*

The worry that was twisting in my stomach rises up in my chest as something darker. I don't think I've ever felt this angry at my aunt. My mom was right. Mimose *can* be selfish.

As I stand here watching her not wonder about me at a time when I've been scared out of my mind, something else occurs to me. Her taking me to Juste's house was foul. Everything could've turned out even worse than it did.

And all this on my birthday.

What's most annoying? My aunt's not even technically here for me to direct all this frustration at. This is Erzu, not Mimose. I doubt I'd even have the courage to confront my aunt if she was here. I've never been angry at her before, so I wouldn't even know how to perform that.

But one thing's for sure: I need to give being angry at her a try. Because I really am cursed, and maybe it's all because of her.

I stomp over to my aunt, take her by the hand, and walk her off the float and onto the curb. She gives me a clumsy hug, throwing her arms around me.

My friends come over, umbrellas closed.

"Have you been playing us this whole time? Just stop it and be real for once," I shout as I work to peel her off me.

"What do you mean?" she mumbles. She's still speaking in her Erzu language. She tries to wipe my cheeks with both her hands. I shake my head out of her grasp and back up.

"Careful," Renee warns me. "Erzu is liable to run away again if we talk harshly to her."

"No. She needs to get it together. I'm tired of this." I look to the woman formerly known as Tati Mimose. "Where's my aunt? Either you, Erzu, know, or you, Mimose, are faking. Yes, you're supposed to be so powerful. How could you let all this happen?"

Erzu/Mimose shrugs and murmurs her answer.

"What do you mean you don't know?" My voice cracks with

emotion, but my shout rises above the thumping music. "Now, enough of this. If it's you, Erzu, I command you out of my aunt. You are not welcome back. If I have any ability to access the power of the bloodline she and I share, I command you *out*."

Suddenly, Erzu abandons her carefree, partying persona. Her spine stretches tall and she adopts the stance of someone sitting on a throne looking down her nose at me. For the first time, her eyes are focused and probing. She parts her lips and utters sounds, which I hear clearly.

I have work to do here.

My words tremble about as much as my body does, but I stand firm. "Why did Juste bring you here? Is he the only one who can remove you?"

I will not leave until my work here is done.

"Stop talking in riddles and tell me what I need to know," I say. "What will it take for you to go away and bring back my aunt?"

One of my powerful children.

I need more answers.

"Which powerful child of yours?" I ask, fresh tears streaming down my face.

But I don't get her reply, because her planets have come for their sun. A group of revelers take Erzu's hand and usher her back to the pavement party.

"I'm with my people, these are my children," she relays to me.

And as I stand there dumbfounded, more of Erzu's dance

partners playfully lead me, and then Kwame, Renee, Sekou, to the party. Before we know it, we are in the center of a dancing mob.

A white cloud of powder closes in on us, and I don't know which way is up.

CHAPTER SEVENTEEN

Shiny faces, swaying hips, bumping booties, and so many colorful flags swarm around me like bees in a bacchanalian hive. People with feathered headdresses dance and hop in celebration all around.

Kofi is the first to grab his phone and record everything in selfie mode. Watching him absorb every second, I think, I want to live in Kofi's Brooklyn. It must be nice.

Renee is in fits of giggles she just can't seem to control. It's hard to tell if it's Sekou's exaggerated moves or this bizarre turn of events. Kwame battles Sekou with his own silly moves, and the two of them break out the Kid 'n Play kick dance. I just know they've done this a million times in their living room.

Someone taps me on my shoulder, and as I turn around, my forehead runs right into Erzu's palm. At first, I think she's checking to see if I have a fever. It makes me wonder whether I look that dazed. Have I tapped into her concern for once?

But when she gives my forehead a little nudge, something happens to me. It's almost like moving through dimensions. Waves of heat emanate from the pavement and rise higher. All the flag colors mixed together begin to look like colorful waves of water. The intense beams of sun dance, distorting everything. The multicolored waves continue to flow until I see what I can only describe as a portal to a clearer vision.

A glimpse of a clear place.

I can make out a circle. I assume it's the makeshift poto-mitan, or pillar, Uncle Rufus mentioned earlier in the park. When I look again, the pillar is a tall tree in the middle of a vast forest. My feet are bare and I walk around the tree once, twice, three times. I feel forced to do this. There is a hateful figure watching and I suddenly feel shame as I walk around the fourth time. This is my penance. My feet follow the worn groove at the base of the tree. Others have been punished in this way. I feel their shame and guilt, too.

I realize that I've circled the tree so many times, I'm confused and it's no longer clear which direction I came from. In a frenzy, I turn from the tree and freak out about finding my way. I look back at the tree, and the groove around it forms a ring that glows and takes the shape of a gold necklace. Grandma Rose's necklace. The pulsating gold glow around it tells me that it's special. Magical.

Go see your mother.

The voice rumbles from the earth beneath my feet.

Go see your mother.

The voice travels from the ground up, coursing through the trunk of the tree. This is the sound of the natural communication network Uncle Rufus spoke about earlier.

Go see your mother.

As the words now release from the treetops, it sounds exactly like Grandma Rose's voice.

Grandma Rose? Is that you?

I search for her, but everything suddenly starts to spin. I see the revelers from the parade. A mix of feathers, flags, and friends. It feels like I'm in orbit and each person is a beam of light. I travel through them, sensing their wonder. But I'm not sure whether my body is standing still or each person is zipping by me. Every hand I grasp in spirit is attached to a soul, each lovingly beckoning me until I tip backward and land back on Eastern Parkway.

Brooklyn.

Earth.

I land in Erzu's arms. Renee rushes over with Kwame.

"Cicely? Are you okay?" Renee asks.

"Let's get her out of here!" shouts Kwame to his brothers. "She needs some air. She needs air."

Kwame, Kofi, Sekou, and Renee find a narrow spot on the curb and help me take sips from a cold bottle of water until I breathe easier again.

Kofi takes out his phone and Kwame issues him a warning. "Kofi, you're not gonna film this, so put that away."

"Don't look at me," Renee laughs when Kwame glances in her direction. "I didn't assign him this beat."

Kofi slowly holds up his hands like he's busted, but then shows his brother the Heart Rate Plus app on his phone screen. "I was just going to check that her pulse is back to normal."

"Aw, that's appreciated." Renee smiles at me reassuringly and then, in the next second, looks around her in a panic. "Oh no. Where's Mimose?"

"Not again," Kofi groans behind a facepalm.

I point to Erzu, who's been leaning against a bus shelter this whole time. Strangely, I get the sense that she's not planning on bolting from here.

Everyone sighs in relief. We are all different types of exhausted, I can tell.

"Can we hang out here just a few minutes longer?" I ask.

"Sure, sis," Renee says.

The affection in her voice puts a lump in my throat. I look from my best friend to Kwame to Kofi to Sekou, the brothers I've come to know today. I want to share what I experienced with them, the way a person tries to recall or share their dream before its memory fades.

"I had this trippy vision, y'all," I start. "And I'm trying to make sense of it."

After explaining everything I felt and saw in detail, I am less shaky and my breathing is back to normal.

"The tree of forgetfulness," Kwame says solemnly. "It's said that as Africans were marched out of their villages by slavers, they were made to walk around a tree several times in the hopes that it caused them to forget their way back home, and also forget their ways."

My face is wet with sorrow as I listen to Kwame. It's new information, yet somehow feels so familiar. The shame I felt in that vision was not of us, but was forced on us. And the fact that it's been passed down is the saddest part of all.

"Home," I say. "That could mean a few things. Like your spiritual center."

Renee nods. "Home is also the most high place where God dwells."

"You both could be saying the same thing, but in a different way," remarks Sekou.

"How about 'home is where the heart is,'" adds Kofi.

Kwame points at him and adds, "Or 'home is where you can completely be yourself.'"

"Those all feel right to me," I say. I stand up slowly. "My aunt has been away too long, and I'm not just talking about today. It's time she finds her way back home. Whatever my mom's reaction to this mess, we have to take Erzu to her. I think it's the only way."

Just as I suspected, Erzu still hasn't moved from her spot.

"She's a lot calmer than she was a few minutes ago," observes Kofi. "That's promising."

Maybe . . .

I run up to her but stop short when my aunt turns to face me. The glazed stare, the slightly dazed look, is undoubtedly Erzu.

"For a second there, I could've sworn she was leaving," I say to no one in particular. "But she's still here."

Whenever it is that we finally get Tati Mimose back, I have a hunch that she'll need the support of her sister. And even though my mom may not admit it, I'm pretty sure she needs her sister just as much.

I loop my arm in Erzu's and we hop on an Um-bro-la ride with my friends over to the Port-au-Princesse booth.

The Port-au-Princesse stand is hoppin'. My dad is at the grill, and my mom just collected money from the last person in line. Satisfied customers are standing around digging into piled-high plates and licking their fingers.

My mom and I lock eyes and I give her a small wave, beckoning her over. The slopes of her brows arch when she reads the worry on my face. She says something to my dad and hands him the customer order slip.

"You never know," Renee tells me. "She may not freak out as hard as you expect."

Erzu slowly turns to look at my mother, who is on her way over here.

"Mimose? What's going on? What's happening?" Mom

232

demands in the key of fed up. Her apron has marinade sauce stains on it, and there are tiny stray balls of tissue along her hairline, from repeated sweat dabbing with thin paper napkins.

There's nothing to do but come clean. Renee, Kwame, Kofi, Sekou, and I all look at one another and nod. Without me asking them to, they stay behind with Erzu as Mom and I walk a few paces away to talk.

I begin, "We need your help."

My mom places her hand on her heart as if to stop it from jumping out of her chest.

I put my hand over hers. "But first let me say, everyone is alive and healthy."

I feel my mom's chest deflate. "Oh, thank the Lord," she breathes. "Amen, Jesus."

I continue, but now my hands are over my own heart. "It's just that something . . . unusual has happened, and I get the feeling that you can help us. Maybe? I didn't know where else to turn."

"Okay, calm down and tell me what happened," Mom says, clearly recovering now that she knows no one has lost their lives today. "I thought Mimose had some interview now with that nineties konpa band. What's she doing here?"

"Nineties band?" I rapid-blink. "Papash wasn't even born back then. Mom, listen—"

"Papash is a kid? It's not the band I used to listen to when I was a teen?" Mom starts singing a few notes like it'll ring a bell for me. "Gade yo, gade yo, gade yo la . . ."

I rub my forehead. My watching friends are picking up that I'm annoyed, and I'm sure they assume it's over my mom's negative reaction. If they only knew. "Uh, no," I say. "Maybe his parents were fans, but I've never heard of that band."

My mom reaches out and affectionately fluffs out some of my coils. "Is that what this is all about? Girl, it's your birthday— if your aunt wants to take you to meet this Papash Junior, of course you can go."

"I can?" I ask, because I didn't expect Mom to be okay with that. This is definitely growth. "Ohmygosh, thank you, Mom!" I give her a hug. "I didn't know how to bring it up, because I know you'd rather I not hang with your sister."

"And I'm sorry my attitude has made you feel that way," Mom says, squeezing me tight. It feels good in her embrace, and I close my eyes. "It's been such a stressful time."

Coming to my senses, I open my eyes, peer over my mom's shoulders, and see my friends heading over with Erzu. They're all smiles, heartened by the sight of this happy hug, obviously thinking they have the all clear. I frantically wave them back.

This not-so-subtle act is not lost on my mother, who pulls away and looks behind her. "But there's something more I need to know, right?"

I take a deep breath and don't stop talking until I've run out of air. "Tati Mimose's client mouth-sprayed ceremonial rum on her and ever since then, she's been possessed with a spirit who's all about smelling and looking good."

Mom erupts like a Caribbean volcano.

"Is this what's been going on all day?" she asks, exasperated. "You lied to me? Why are you just now telling me this?"

"I didn't know how you would take it and I thought I could handle it on my own," I say.

"Well, you clearly did not handle it. And you know how I feel about your dabbling in things you know nothing about!" Mom chides me. She shakes her head. "This is so typical of Mimose. She's been exposing you to this business since before you could even ride a bike!" She shuts her eyes and wipes her forehead with the napkin she's clutching. Her face is clear of any napkin residue now.

"Is Vodou what you're talking about, Mom? Is that what you're talking around? You can say the word, you know. And for the record, it doesn't scare me and I'm not cursed."

"Don't be ridiculous," Mom spits back. "And so what if maybe I'm tiptoeing a little bit around *Vodou*?"

Understatement of the year. But there's no time right now to debate this position.

I heave out a breath. "Mom, I know you're angry at Mimose for all the things she's done in the past, but she needs you now," I plead. "We've collected the items for the de-possession, but we fell short of securing a priestess. We've hit a brick wall and need help."

My mom doesn't look the least bit moved by my words. "Funny how I have to always be the one to drop everything and pick up the pieces after Mimose breaks something."

"That's because she can count on you." That crackle of emotion is back in my voice. Every part of me is vibrating with desperation. I stand here unsure if I have the skill to pry the lock off my mom's heart when it comes to her kid sister. I take a deep breath and think of Grandma Rose. If there's any part of her that is still with us, I hope she can guide me into that locked part of my mom's heart.

"Mimose . . . she lost her mom, too," I say in a small voice. "And you're pretty much the closest thing each other has. To be honest, it's a lot of pressure, being the reason why you stay mad at each other."

Mom's eyes switch to soft focus like she's reflecting on my words. I do the fourth-grade thing and cross my fingers, hoping she agrees to help. She opens her mouth to say something, and I lean in.

"Margo!" Dad shouts from the grill in an overwhelmed voice. "Someone's ready to order—a little help with this customer, please!"

Sekou heads over to my dad. "I can help if you need a hand."

Mom manages to crack a smile. "Oh, thank you, son. God bless you. Mr. Destin will tell you how you can help."

"Does that mean you'll help us?" I ask Mom.

"Of course I'll handle this," she answers, as if there was never any doubt. "That's what families do."

I lead my mom over to where Renee, Kwame, and Kofi are keeping Erzu distracted with a TikTok dance lesson.

I'm about to ask Mom what she'll do when I hear a familiar voice that fills me with dread.

"Port-au-Princesse."

My fingers drum on my mother's arm in alert before I can get the words out. My reflexes don't kick in as quickly as I need them to.

"Mommy, that's him!"

Juste blocks our path, holding up the Port-au-Princesse flyer for us to see. "Found you."

CHAPTER EIGHTEEN

With one sweeping motion of her strong, protective arm, Mom gathers me behind her and away from Juste. She leans toward him and freezes him with an icy stare. "What do you want with my sister?" she demands.

"Your sister?" Juste's eyes bulge and redden with fury. "It's you. You've cursed me. From the start."

Incredulous, I step from behind my mother. "What are you talking about? My mom doesn't even know you!"

I look to my mother. "Right, Mom? Tell him."

She looks shiftier than a Prospect Park squirrel.

"Oh, she knows me," Juste says, "and I wish I never laid eyes on her."

My friends take notice of Juste on the scene and they rush over to help. Bad idea. This only brings Tati Mimose within arm's reach of Juste.

Mom finally speaks. "You're not welcome here. Turn around, and head back where you came from."

Whatever my mom's secrets, I can't help but stan her unrelenting queen flex right now.

"Don't worry, I'm not dumb enough to eat even a crumb from you," Juste spits. "But first I need Erzulie to do something for me."

In one swift motion, Juste reaches for the back pocket of his baggy shorts. We all recoil out of fear, not knowing his intentions. He can pull anything out of there, from a weapon to a magic show bunny.

I'm sure no one suspects that he'll pull out a bottle of rum like he does. Juste takes a swig and then spews out the rum, which showers over Erzu.

A commotion of "No!" and "Stop!" break out, and a wet-faced Erzu falters like she's going to pass out. Kwame and I help Renee and my mother hold Erzu up. Kofi grabs a bottle of water from his supply backpack in case this is just Erzu on heat exhaustion and not on more of Juste's sorcery.

"Stand back!" my mother warns Juste, who is approaching us like a predator lured by the sight of a wounded animal.

"No, you stand back," he growls, coming closer. "I'm going to fix what you started. I'm going to get my life back on track."

Mom keeps her eye on Juste even while clutching her drowsy kid sister. "I have nothing to do with your life getting off track. Stop making excuses and make the life you want."

"Nothing is ever your fault!" shouts Juste, who is now prowling the perimeter of our Erzu cluster. If we give him a hole, he'll reach in and snatch Erzu from us, I can tell. "You can't deny what you did. Erzulie's going to help me. And I won't let you get in my way."

"Give me everything you collected for the priestess." My mother looks stone-faced, holding out her hand to Renee. She flutters her fingers, signaling for Renee to hurry.

Who, what, when, where, why is Mom . . . ? "But . . . what are—" I ask, because is this an act? Is she trying to fake Juste out, hoping he leaves before she has to actually do anything?

"Just do it!" Mom commands. "Douse the herbs with Florida Water."

Wait. That sounds like what Uncle Rufus said gets done during Vodou ceremonies. Could be my mom just googled it once.

One person is buying this wholesale. When he sees what's going on, worry gnarls Juste's face. "Get out of my way."

"Go get my dad!" I shout to Kofi.

"No, there's no need for that," comes a booming voice.

A beautiful tall man dressed as a warrior swoops in. It's Dresden, Tati Mimose's could-be boyfriend and apparent Brooklyn superhero.

He's even got that superhero banter going. "It looks like my hunger struck me just in time," he says, flyer in hand. "I came here to check out Port-au-Princesse, but it looks like you've got unwanted company. Anything I can do to help?"

Dresden stands facing Juste, arms at his sides like a warrior at the ready.

"Listen, you Black Panther movie extra," says Juste with extra bass in his voice. "This ain't Hollywood. This is Brooklyn, and you don't know what you're messing with. Step aside."

"I don't think you really want some of this. Bullies like you don't usually pick on someone their own size."

As afraid of a Wakanda-sized beatdown as Juste may be, he still steps toward Dresden. But right before any blows are thrown, Erzu's gang of costumed dancers flood the area and form a wall circling us, separating us from Juste.

Kwame reaches for my free hand and we look at each other in amazement. The dancers all form a joyous, laughing, singing, Caribbean-flags-waving barrier. It faces outward and it's impenetrable. Nothing can get through.

Dresden is in the circle with us, and he keeps eye on the crowd and on Juste.

"Make sure no one is filming or taking pictures of this," says my mom. "Even though I'm sure Erzulie wouldn't mind the attention, we do."

Erzulie. That's the correct name I couldn't get right when Juste first said it. Maybe not so deep down, I was being cautious with the name, unsure of what saying it repeatedly all day would invoke. Calling the spirit *Erzu* was my fail-safe.

Kofi, Kwame, and Renee join Dresden in his watch. My mom and I crouch down and I lean Erzu against me for support. I watch in awe as my mom gets to work. All the supplies are lined up next to Renee's bag—rum, the hex pouch, Florida Water, the medicinal plant, the fetish, the mojo bone, and the rosary beads.

Clutching the Florida Water–soaked plant, Mom looks at the backs of the people in the human wall around us. "This is a joyous time; we need some singing."

"Hey, Renee, let's do it," I shout.

My bestie looks back and nods at me, understanding exactly what I mean. Together, we lead the crowd in in singing "Sensational."

Island, inland, shared land, ONE / Represent the Caribbe-AN / See, hear, smell, taste bacchan-AL / Our vibes dem so SENSEsation-AL!

Mom begins to recite prayers to open what I gather is the type of ceremony Juste had been hoping Tati Mimose would perform when we went to his place what feels like a lifetime ago. My mind is blown at this glimpse of a very different side of my mom.

She asks Kofi to get her a lit candle and a pan from her booth and he's back with them in a flash. I guess the candle was one list item we missed.

"Help her to her feet," Mom instructs Renee and me.

Erzu calmly sways side to side like a palm tree on a windy day, but we get her to stand. Mom touches Erzu's shoulders with the soaked plant like the queen of England might touch a sword to the shoulders of one being bestowed with knighthood. Could she be cleansing her aura? All the while, Mom prays, "We thank you for being here and for your protection and guidance on this day.

We release you from this plane. And as we send you on your journey, we welcome back our sister Mimose."

I can see now that Mom is wearing the rosary around her neck. The cross pendant dangles, glinting in the sun. Using the string from the hex pouch, she ties the pendant to the fetish and mojo bone. Mom holds the bundle against Mimose's forehead and then her chest and shoulders in the sign of the cross. She repeats the motion over and over while reciting the same prayer.

This is beyond shocking, and honestly I don't know how I'm keeping my composure so well. Other than my mouth remaining in a gaping position, and besides almost choking on my own saliva, I'd say I haven't overreacted to this bombshell of a revelation.

Is this really my mom? Could it be possible that she is the priestess we'd been searching all of Brooklyn for? I don't even know how this could be. When did she learn all this and why did she hide her knowledge from me? How is it that she dogs everything related to Vodou and yet she clearly practices it? Is this like when those moral-high-ground politicians get their shocking dirty laundry aired?

Finally, Mom pours some rum into the pan and touches the candle to it. When the blue flames rise from the pan, Mom transfers the rosary beads to Tati Mimose. Erzu stays calm as my mom places it around her neck.

Erzu's head drops forward, lifts, and drops forward again, but I continue singing "Sensational." Mom repeats the prayer, which she utters more forcefully with every round. The singing, too, becomes more rousing, and lively and punctuated by hand-clapping. Erzu gets swept up by the sounds. She goes from swaying to spinning and dancing, until she goes off balance and falls into me. As I steady her, she grabs me by my shoulders and her eyes meet mine.

That's when I see it. That unmistakable quirk to her eyebrow, that singular smirk I've seen a million times. But it's mostly in the eyes. The fathomless, knowing eyes where I've found solace and understanding and concern and love my entire life.

"Grandma Rose?"

CHAPTER NINETEEN

I am still suspended in disbelief when her words reach my heart in a voice so familiar, so distinct. "Your birthday wish guided me here, and I traveled on the only day I could."

The earth under me shifts and knocks my heart into a free fall. I hold on tight to the figure in front of me. Then a cool whoosh of air fans my skin, leaving goose bumps in its path.

"Grandma Rose!"

It was my grandmother the entire time and not a Vodou spirit? What about the fact that Juste sprayed rum on my aunt after he called for Erzulie?

The questions swirling in my mind knock my world upside down. It is all so disorienting and confusing. This feeling is familiar, and I remember my vision.

The gleaming gold necklace! Grandma's gold necklace.

A calm comes over me as all the puzzle pieces suddenly fall into place. I'm back at that moment I handed Tati Mimose the gold necklace to hold in her pouch. The rush of wind that knocked her off balance. She was wobbly even as we climbed the stairs to Juste's place.

"Juste didn't cause this," I say aloud. *My grandmother did.*

I've heard Tati Mimose's jokes before, about Grandma Rose being the embodiment of one of the spirits Tati honors. Erzu's love of adornment and fragrance and flair mirrors my grandmother's. But I never made the connection because I didn't really understand the reference. Who was Erzu? I guess it was a nickname for my ghostly grandmother.

Grandma Rose came here to mend the family, but I assigned her another purpose entirely. Could it be my nagging concerns over how my mom or Renee or the dollar-van passenger see Vodou that had me warping my own perceptions of Vodou? Could it be my grandmother was counting on being mistaken for Erzu? If not, how else would we have learned how similar my mom and Mimose truly are?

Juste was the one who identified my grandmother as a spirit. And Erzu shared the same showy characteristics and penchant for fragrances and jewelry as my grandmother. So I just went with the spirit being Erzu. I didn't question it—sort of like the way I went with thinking the dollar-van driver's name was Rasta. But knowing my crafty grandma, she let this perception work in her favor. I don't know if I could've handled knowing Erzu was really Grandma Rose at the same time I was discovering my other-worldly translation skills.

As I clutch the essence of Grandma Rose housed in Tati Mimose, I begin to understand. Generations ago, when a stolen people were barbarically shipped as cargo from their homeland to a foreign land, the spirits traveled with them. The spirits, with their humanlike qualities—flaws, foibles, and all. It's what makes the spirits relatable and helpful, even.

When families and culture were stripped from the stolen people and the tongues in their very mouths were made to twist around words so foreign to them, they were able to communicate, practice their ways, and connect with the familiar through the spirit guardians. Generations later, the children of the stolen may not store these memories in their brains, but they are imprinted in their minds. Though they have no knowledge of these practices, they carry a knowing of them.

My mind reviews the day in search of the clues I missed, and I don't notice Mom is now at my side until Grandma Rose links my hand to Mom's. Mom's face is already streaming with tears. She knows. God. She knows.

Our hands are joined in a family circle when Grandma Rose's lips deliver a message in an otherworldly language.

I translate aloud for my mother: "There's a beautiful home waiting on the other side, but for here, that home is in the bonds we share. Never lose your connection to that home, no matter how far you roam or how many times you circle that tree."

And with that, Grandma Rose nods in farewell. Mom and I

tearfully return her nod before her head falls forward, the weight of it slumping her shoulders. Her knees buckle, and Mom and I catch her.

"Will she be okay?" I choke.

A peaceful calm reshapes my mom's features as she tells me, "They both will be okay, baby. They both will."

The weight in our arms shifts and slips and we call for help. In a beat, Kwame is at my side. When we all gaze down, we're sure the spirit inhabiting this body belongs to none other than Tati Mimose.

She blinks lazily and puts weight on her own two feet. Wobbly at first but getting steadier by the second. We gently release her arm.

She whips her head back to me and gives me a knowing smile with a wink. Obviously approving of Kwame.

"He's cute," she says.

I shake my head and let out a hearty laugh that brings bitter-sweet tears to my eyes. "Welcome back."

Tati Mimose is clearly disoriented, trying to get her sea legs. She pats her outfit and her hair. And then for the first time, she notices my mother's presence.

"What are you doing here?" Tati Mimose asks, confused.

"Oh, just dabbling a little. You understand."

My aunt notices the supplies strewn around our feet and asks, "Margo, what are you even doing with this stuff? Isn't it sacrilege?"

"It's culture," answers Mom through a twisted pout. "It's something born out of necessity, and so I was doing what I needed to do, just off my instincts."

I cough out a laugh, incredulous. "My mom was the priestess we needed all along," I announce.

Sekou's friend's observation from this morning comes to me. *I guess real Gs move in silence.*

Tati Mimose rapid-blinks. It's obvious she's got so many questions and doesn't know where to begin. "But why didn't you ever tell me? You could've helped others."

"I'm helping in my own way," says Mom.

I have questions, too. So I pose one to her. "Did you perform a ceremony for Juste or something?"

Mom looks at me. "Years ago I helped Juste's girlfriend with career advice. And prayer. She got an opportunity and moved cross-country. But if you ask me, Juste needs a ceremony. I can tell he's possessed with the spirit of obsession."

"Who taught you how to do all this?" Tati Mimose asks.

Mom shrugs a shoulder. "It was born in me."

I throw up my hands. "But I've never seen you practice Vodou!" I say. "You've always seemed like you're against that. Why is that?"

Mom opens her mouth to speak and then closes it again. Words form on her next attempt, though they tumble out slowly. "To tell you the truth, I don't ever think I fully unpacked why I feel uncomfortable with Vodou," she tells me. "At first, it was a knee-jerk response, maybe based on how other people or the church view Vodou. I accepted this view. And I wanted you to stay away from it for the same reason," she tells me. "And I did this all without interrogating my response. You're interrogating and unpacking deeper than I ever did, and I respect that. I won't say that I don't still hope you stay away from Vodou, but I admire you for not accepting wholesale what you're fed. I admire your aunt for the same reason."

Even though I can tell my mom is choosing her words carefully so as not to come across too judgmental, I don't think I've ever heard her speak so sincerely about Vodou. I can't stop a lump from forming in my throat. Both my mom and Tati Mimose have glassy eyes.

"Thanks, Mom," I finally say.

"Shoot, I still can't get over the fact that you're a natural," Mimose tells Mom, falling back into their sibling banter, which I've missed hearing for too long. "I've read about people like you, who are rare, by the way. I worked so hard learning about traditional ceremonies. You wake up like this."

"Why do you work so hard at it? You have gifts that come naturally to you. Look around," Mom says. Tati Mimose glances up and smiles at the wall of people around us. "See how many people are here for you? I wish I could just wake up like that. I know where my strengths are, and that's what I focus on."

"I'm so sorry about this, Margo," croaks Tati Mimose.

"See what happens when I leave my child with you? Hmm." Mom pouts.

My aunt looks nervous and I flash back to that moment when I was nine. That moment when my mother was last glowering at her sister. I gulp.

Mom speaks slowly and intentionally. She looks her sister in the eyes and I brace myself. "Mimose, you're the best aunt Cicely could ever ask for. I was just upset because I wanted Cicely to keep the same distance away from Vodou as I do. Maybe I could tell she is naturally drawn to it, and I didn't want it to be true. I regret keeping Cicely apart from you, and I'm sorry I got between you two. That was terrible of me," says Mom with a hitch in her voice. She turns to look at me now. "And, Cicely baby, I'm so sorry. That was wrong and I promise to do better."

I feel a lump in my throat. Mimose's eyes twinkle with tears.

Mom gives her sister a quick hug and then pulls back. "How about I keep the home fires burning for you at our family church, and you keep the home fires burning around that poto-mitan?" Mom waits for Tati Mimose's choked-up nod, and the sisters hug again, before Mom pulls away. "Enough of this, you're probably running late for your interview, and I need to get back to the grill."

That conversation did for my emotional well-being what the herbs do for people spiritually. I feel cleansed, and I'm grateful to my grandmother, to the spirits, and to God for it.

I blink and look around. "Where's Juste?" I ask my friends.

Renee sucks her teeth as she walks over to us with Kofi. "Oh, that dude? Homie realized he's no match for you powerful women."

"He probably caught the last time machine back to the nineties," jokes Kofi.

The crowd has gone back to partying freestyle, and Mom joins my dad at their stand.

I put my arm around Tati Mimose and face my friends. "Uh, Kwame, Kofi, I want to introduce you to my real aunt."

"Nice to meet you," says Kwame.

"I can't believe I'm going to say this, but I think I'm gonna miss Erzu," admits Renee. "But hi there, real auntie."

Mimose smiles and waves to Renee, Kwame, and Kofi.

"Where were you all this time?" Kofi boldly asks the question on all of our minds. Kwame shoots him one of his warning glares, but he leans in to hear my aunt's answer at the same time.

Tati Mimose yawns and stretches her arms and body as if she's just rolled out of bed. "It's hard to explain, but I feel relaxed, sort of like when I fall asleep while getting a massage at the spa."

She shrugs, and Dresden comes over and helps her when she takes a wobbly step. She thanks him and they hold each other's gaze for a few seconds.

I clear my throat. "Tati Mimose, only you can make a totally zany situation seem glamorous."

"So, this thing with Papash . . ." says Tati Mimose, gnawing on her lower lip.

"Last we heard he was running late for the interview," Renee tells her.

Kwame chimes in. "And we saw him on a float a little while ago."

I take a chance and ask, "Did you know the podcast lined up all these Hollywood Vodou–themed sponsors?" I ask.

"Yes," she says.

"Don't you think that's a little . . . distasteful?" I am careful not to accuse her of selling out. At least not before I hear her explanation.

Dresden smiles that brilliant smile of his, and it nearly blinds us. "These kids obviously don't have to pay rent."

"What's that supposed to mean?" I challenge him.

Tati Mimose cuts in. "I was going to make the Vodou movie a topic of our discussion. The podcast bosses didn't know that, but I don't care. My mission is to be a cultural ambassador, and I know that as more people become aware of Vodou, there can be more instances of appropriation. Like the way Hollywood takes on zombie tales. But I won't stop challenging perceptions about Vodou in a responsible way, and if I get paid to do that, I'm for it."

"I guess things aren't always how we perceive them," says Kwame with a glance at me.

"Thanks for explaining that," I say to my aunt. "I may

not understand it a hundred percent, but I understand you."

"And thank you all for protecting me even though you didn't totally understand what was happening. If I knew this interview was still happening, I'd reward you all with a Papash selfie," says Tati Mimose. "I was looking forward to meeting him myself."

I'm relieved to hear Tati Mimose say that.

As I glance around at the crowd, I get a sudden idea. "Well, you already have an audience. You can conduct your own podcast interview if you call him. I have his number. Papash's number. In my phone." I don't think I'll ever get used to saying that.

Tati Mimose nods. "You know what, that's not a bad idea." She looks in her fanny pack. "Do you, or anybody, have my phone?"

I grab it from my back pocket and hand it to her. Then I text her Papash's number, and I look on in amazement as my aunt casually *texts Papash*.

"All set," she says after a minute. "We're going to do our interview on Instagram Live."

Renee jumps into breaking-news action. "Once you go live, I'll tag the podcast to alert them of this new direction."

IG livestream cued up, Tati Mimose takes center stage from the streets of Brooklyn.

"Hello. Welcome to Carnival! Brooklyn's West Indian Day Parade is a tradition that we hold dear. A lot of my followers are outside of the metro area may not have attended before, so let me break it down for you how crucial and how dazzling Carnival is. It's a place where we come together to celebrate triumph, survival, and culture. It's about stripping away the limits we place on ourselves. We're here to celebrate as ourselves and our ancestors. To celebrate the entire of the human condition—including our pains, our joys, all rolled into one."

The crowd cheers and gets into formation around her. I feel my heart swell with pride. This is the Mimose I know and love.

"On this day," Mimose continues, "everything is two sides of the same coin. Who I express myself to be today, and who I really am at my core. The two sides come out and they dance together, in all of their complexity. And yes, there are things that we choose to do in order to survive. In order to be accepted and to be seen. But what's driving us is the true self within that is always stirring. It's the engine that gives us energy to face another day. And no, there is no shame in that. And no, we are not cursed with this existence, but blessed with it."

Renee reaches for my hand and squeezes it. I look at her watery eyes and can't help my tears from falling once again. We break from our hug when we notice Tati Mimose pausing to steady her breath. Her voice is quivering and I wonder if she's thinking this idea was a mistake. When she glances at me, I give her a thumbs-up and keep-going nod.

"Party people, just like you, I have visions and goals. I want to teach and preserve our spiritual legacies. How about we check in with Brooklyn's biggest teen rapper, Papash, and find out how his vision and goals led him to the top spot on playlists?"

Everyone around my aunt cheers, including me and Renee.

"Now . . ." Tati Mimose pauses and taps a button on her phone. "Yes, Papash, you may join my livestream. Everyone, welcome to the very first Mimose Benoirs Show and our first guest, Papash!"

We cannot contain ourselves. I scream so loud, I get a headache. This is a Caribbean Christmas beyond my wildest dreams. But somehow, everyone calms down soon enough to listen in. Renee and I step off to one side to watch the live chat on my phone.

My aunt gets Papash to open up on a topic I've never heard him talk about—spirituality and its role in his career. People chime in with their questions. Shout-outs are made. And it's a beautiful thing.

After they wrap up the interview, Papash signs off with his trademark dreamy smile.

"One more thing," Mimose says. "If you are here at the parade today, please do stop by the Port-au-Princesse booth and enjoy authentic, delicious Haitian dishes. My very own sister runs this amazing restaurant. Port-au-Princesse also has a real brick-and-mortar location near the Junction on Glenwood, and I hope to catch you there too sometime."

I gasp with joy. My aunt's shout-out is going to make such a difference for my parents' restaurant. I can practically sense people in the crowd already making their way to the booth.

Suddenly, I see that Mimose is waving me over to her. I close out of the app on my phone and walk over to join my aunt, feeling a little shy. She wraps an arm around me and pulls me into the frame with her.

"I'm really excited that you could join me, everyone!" Mimose goes on. "We are live here at Brooklyn's Labor Day Parade with some of my most favorite people, including my niece, who I want to wish a happy birthday today!"

The applause that breaks out for me is awkward enough to endure. But when my aunt leads everyone in the "Happy Birthday" song, I really don't know what to do with my hands.

"Happy birthday to youuu!" the crowd begins.

I grin the whole time I'm showered with singing and best wishes. Everyone dances around me, and this time I'm not feeling lightheaded or tired. I feel just right. And I dance along.

After Tati Mimose logs off from her live, I thank her for the birthday shout-out. She shakes her head.

"I promised you'd get to meet Papash on your birthday," she says, texting someone again. "And I like to keep my promises."

I'm about to ask my aunt what she means when I hear the unmistakable sample from one very famous blockbuster.

"Here comes the *Black Panther*–themed float!" Renee calls, pointing down Eastern Parkway.

I run over to join her, Kwame, and Kofi. Kwame's grinning.

"Now's your chance to impress them, Kwame," says Kofi.

I jump up and down in anticipation, glad Kwame gets the chance to see this mas camp.

"Shall I still audition for this right here and now?" he shouts back.

"Yes, and I'll be your partner if you need one," I tell him.

Kwame gives me a playful shoulder bump. I look up at his brown eyes and smile.

"You ready?" he asks me. I nod, and he links his fingers through mine just as the Dora Milaje and their Wakandan brethren arrive. Their appearance just about tears the roof off every building on the Parkway. Kwame faces me and starts jumping up and down instead of wining. I cheer as I jump, too. We jump and dance as hard as the soca drums ring out.

This is what I love about Carnival. All of us give out and get as much energy as each truck comes. It's a classic exchange, a call-and-response communication that keeps us bonded through generations. No translator needed. Because at the heart of it all is a language we all understand—a love we have for one another, which makes this celebration feel amazing.

After the Wakanda float has passed, Kwame and I step to the sidelines and take a moment to catch our breaths.

"So . . . there's something you should know about me," he confesses.

"Will it change my mind about you?" I tease.

"It might," he answers with a cringe.

"Lay it on me."

"You sure?" He winces.

"Very," I answer.

"Cicely Destin, my name is Kwame Hilliard and I am . . ." he mumbles.

I grin at his clowning and say, "Don't be a nincompoop. Speak up!"

"I am . . ." He mumbles again in a way my powers of communication can't access.

"One more time for the people out in Jersey?"

"I'm *corny*, aight? I'm a certified cornball."

I shrug. "Hey, you are who you are. And it's a good look on you."

"You're really magical, you know that?" he says, his presence warming me. The soothing notes in his voice strike those tingly sensations up and down my spine.

"Are you talking about my translation gift?" I ask.

I don't know how I'd answer this question, because I'm still processing it myself—the fact that I could understand Erzu. For now, I think I'll practice the type of communication that trees have—a compassionate and organic one. I don't know how many ways this gift will express itself, but if I can use it to help others, I will.

"Not just the translation gift," answers Kwame. "Your presence in general."

"Thank you," I tell him, my heart racing.

"And since we're talking about *presence* and gifts . . . I wanted to say happy birthday again."

"Okay, that *was* pretty corny." I grin. "And to be clear, there's nothing wrong with that."

"Good," he says. "Happy birthday, Cicely."

He steps forward and gives me a hug, sending my heart plink-plinking like a steel drum.

It takes everything in my power not to do something goofy to break the mood, like slap him on the back for fun. When he ends the hug, he doesn't step away. His fingers find mine and we keep them interlaced. His face is so close to mine. And I meet him when he leans in close, and I kiss him back just as sweetly when his lips touch mine.

My first kiss.

Right now is the only moment like this moment.

I don't know how long Kwame and I stand there, kissing, but I'm vaguely aware of people cheering. Oh no. Has everyone seen us? Kofi better not be filming this. Kwame and I break apart, and it's only then that I see the familiar chrome-plated truck we saw earlier, coming up the parkway. It's Papash's float! And . . . it's coming to a stop?

"Here's our ride," Mimose says, giving me and Kwame a quick wink. "Come on!" she hollers to Renee and Kofi, who come running.

"We're going to get on Papash's float?" I ask my aunt, stunned. She nods, beaming at me.

Renee and I clutch each other's hands and search each other's faces in disbelief.

"This is really happening!" we yell.

I feel like I've ascended. I will never fully come back down and be grounded after this.

Before we know it, security guards are guiding us aboard the float, one at a time.

We climb chrome stairs and then we scale the speakers. When we reach the top, Papash is there with his arms out-stretched to us.

"This is my niece, Cicely," Mimose tells Papash proudly.

"Yes, happy birthday," he says in greeting, and holds his arms out to *me*.

Speechless, I walk into Papash's embrace.

Papash's embrace!

Time screeches to a halt. I glance at Kwame to see if he's jealous, but he's grinning big. And I realize that as amazing as Papash is, it's Kwame I'm excited to dance with later.

Renee takes a million pictures of me with Papash, and I do the same for her. Next, Papash invites me and Mimose to wave a Haitian flag at the front of the truck. Tati Mimose is at my side, helping me wave the banner and pump up the crowd.

Never in my entire life have I ridden atop a truck at the parade. The view from this height takes my breath away. All of Eastern Parkway is laid out before us, and the massive million-strong crowd is fully hyped by Papash's presence. When the beat to "Sensational" drops, we all lose our minds and shake up the entire parade route. I suspect we all won't come down from this spiritual high for at least the rest of the school year.

Do-over challenge, devoured. Plate licked clean.

CHAPTER TWENTY

That night, we all gather on Tati Mimose's rooftop for an impromptu post parade party. Everyone is here—including my parents. It's the perfect open-air setting under the stars that feels like the best way to wind down after a supercharged day. The jazzy music playing from the speakers is as cooling as the night breeze.

And the best part might be the food: leftovers from a place called Port-au-Princesse, where the service is compassionate and the food is bussin bussin.

"Yo, where did you say your mom's shop is at again?" Kofi asks, totally pumped, as he scarfs down his plate of rice and peas. He, Kwame, Renee, and I are sitting on plastic chairs in a semi-circle. My aunt is hanging out with my parents on the other side of the rooftop. It's been forever since I've seen my mom and her sister party together, and I watch them with joy. Then I turn back to Kofi.

"I'll text you and Kwame the address," I tell him.

Kwame closes his eyes as he savors the flavor of the beef cube he's just popped into his mouth. "Oh yes, we're going there tomorrow after school," he vows.

Renee has no qualms about talking with her mouth full when she needs to say something urgent. "If you're gonna hang out there, buy something more than just a drink."

"We got you," says Kwame, and Kofi nods enthusiastically.

Sekou walks over to join our group with his own plate. "Smelling that food all day without eating was torture!"

I could be wrong, but suddenly Renee is not in any rush to talk while chewing. She swallows everything down and then asks, "How did you like working for Mr. and Ms. Destin at their booth today?"

He smiles sweetly at Renee. Hmm. My sixth sense is picking up on something, but for now, I'll just see how it all unfolds.

"They're cool people," Sekou says. "I'm going to be working at the restaurant some weekends."

We all congratulate Sekou on his new gig. He seems more relaxed as he pulls up a chair between Kwame and Kofi. I watch as the brothers interact, teasing one another, the way my mom and aunt are talking over each other right now; I see them out of the corner of my eye. I absorb all I can and pay attention to the nonverbal communication I pick up on. I realize that every laugh shared is an act of forgiveness.

"I'm not worried about it," Kofi is saying. "I know I'll ace that entrance exam, so just save me a seat next year at Christian Prep."

Sekou hoots and turns to Kwame. "That means you need to step up your academic game, or Kofi will be tutoring you soon."

"Oh, I'm not worried, either," answers Kwame.

I guess that means Kwame will be raising his hand more in class. I think deep down he's grateful knowing that he can share more of his authentic self in the future.

That's the magic of Carnival. The feel-good vibes generated at the parade linger and last for a long time. It's the best kind of aftertaste. Every *tink* of the steel pan, every thump from the subwoofers, every wine of the hips and body slam of the mosh pit is a boost to the island spirit that stays with you. At school, when you're handed your test, you want to wave it like a flag. When you're walking the busy halls, you want to run up on someone and dance with them. In the cafeteria, heading for a meal, you want to ask for Cola Couronne. When you hear the school bell, it sounds like a J'Ouvert whistle.

"What are you smiling at?" Renee asks me.

I turn to her. "You ever notice that tough conversations reveal the flip sides of the stories that we tell ourselves?"

Renee tilts her head to one side. "I've been thinking along those lines today," she says. She takes a swig of her water and looks at the string of white headlights on the road below us. "It was a lot for me, everything with Mimose."

"I know," I tell her.

"But if I want to be a journalist, I need to keep an open mind, even about stuff I don't understand."

"Even about stuff you don't agree with," I offer with a knowing look.

She winces. "Was it that obvious?"

I shrug. "I maybe picked up on some of your . . . discomfort."

Renee fills her cheeks with air before blowing it out. "I'm sorry about the shade, and I'm sorry for how that must've made you feel."

"The discomfort, I expect and understand," I explain. "But it also seemed like you were . . . a little ashamed."

Renee hangs her head. "I felt ashamed that I was ashamed, and that spiral only stopped when I just focused on our mission."

"No, I get it." I give Renee's arm a gentle rub, grateful we didn't let the day's rifts tear a hole in our friendship; we let it stretch instead. "And hearing you talk about this stuff kinda helps me understand a bit more about how my mom must feel."

Renee nods and meets my gaze. "All I know is when I go for the school paper's editor spot, I want to tell stories that give context and report on all angles of a subject."

"I love it—those are the stories I need to read."

"What about you? Any new year's resolutions?" she asks.

"Hmmm . . . besides keeping my phone off in class?" I laugh. "When things are not what we think they are, I'll listen closer. I'll try to adopt a more panoramic view of everything."

"Ooh, how about we make that our friendship creed?" Renee smiles.

"Agreed."

We link pinkies.

"Waddup, cuzzz!" a girl shrieks at top volume. I nearly drop my plate and turn in my seat to see my two cousins from Jersey running over to me.

"Gabby! Simone!" I shout, jumping up. The three of us hug one another like we did when we were little. "You're here!"

Simone grins. "We wouldn't miss your birthday and Labor Day for the world."

I let her words sink in. It really all happened today. My birthday. The Labor Day Parade. My Caribbean Christmas.

"We saw you on Papash's float at the parade!" Gabby exclaims. "OMG. We tried to find you after, but it was too crowded. You've got to tell us everything."

I shake my head, not even knowing where to start. Then a cute boy appears behind Simone, putting his arm around her. Simone beams and introduces me to her boyfriend, Ben. I remember my manners and introduce everyone sitting in the circle—though my cousins know Renee, of course. When I introduce Kwame, Simone double-eye-winks at me.

"Cicely," my mom calls out from where she's standing with my aunt and my dad. "Come here!"

"Margo's daugh-tah," Renee and I pretend-shout at the same

time. We holler with laughter, and everyone else looks at us like we've lost it.

I make my way to my family. Mom is holding out a satiny birthday sash and puts it around me.

"I forgot to give you this earlier today," she says.

"Aw, and it's in Haitian colors, which I love," I say. Dad urges me to pose for a picture and I do. After my solo pic, Mom jumps in for a pic with me.

"Mimose, get in here!" Mom calls.

Tati Mimose walks over. "I believe this belongs to you," she tells me, placing Grandma Rose's gold necklace around my neck.

Once it's clasped, I pretend to lose my footing. Tati Mimose steadies me in a faux panic, and we both laugh and shake our heads.

Necklace secured, my mom and aunt sandwich me in for a group pic. And I can't get over how amazing it feels to have my birthday wish come true—here I am, a bridge between my mom and my aunt.

I guess I come from a line of sensational women who have special sight, and a special ear. And now I know that's something I want to cultivate.

"Thank you, fam. Thanks for everything," I say.

Just then, a tall, handsome guy my aunt's age walks in through the door to the rooftop. It's Dresden! My heart skips a beat when I see Dresden come over to greet Tati Mimose, and she smiles at him. He's a good guy. And they make a cute couple.

My phone buzzes with an alert. Someone named Aleta has just DM'ed me. I have no idea who that is, until I see her profile picture. It's the woman I met earlier today—Grandma Rose's former art student. *Wow. She really followed through and reached out.*

I read her message: *Swing by our creative co-working sessions any time you're in the mood to take your copy/pasting to the next level. You're always welcome.* There's a post she's shared that lists the open gallery hours.

Bet.

It feels like that seeded thought planted in my mind earlier has started to sprout. And for some reason, I can't stop smiling.

Someone puts on a soca song, and before the beat even drops, everyone is their feet. I rejoin Renee, Kwame, Kofi, Sekou, Simone, Gabby, and Ben, and we all start dancing. Simone and Ben do the Haitian two-step together, and they look so in love. Kwame spins me around and I smile, remembering our dreamy kiss. I can't wait to kiss him again.

As I dance with my crew, I dance for my blessings. I dance with intention. I dance with hope and purpose in mind. The next time my first day looks like it's destined for doom, I will remind myself that I am not cursed; I am experiencing all the flavors and colors of this life. And if I focus on the gloomy side of things, I'll never notice the brighter moments. Even if I encounter a place where evil resides, I will know that good lies under that same roof.

I glance up at the night sky and the vast expanse of stars. There are so many versions of ourselves to discover. There are also more secrets to uncover, however scary or taboo they may be. I'm ready to learn more about my traditions, and I know that Grandma Rose—and maybe a couple of helpful spirits—will be guiding me every step of the way.

But right now, I'm just going to enjoy being fifteen. Because, so far, it's off to a good start.

AUTHOR'S NOTE

Writing this book was tough for me. Not so much because of the usual wrestle-with-self that comes with authoring. It was the fear of what my family would think of me penning a book about a taboo topic like Vodou. Unfortunately, that fear was stronger than the worry over what my editor, Aimee Friedman, would think of me for not turning in my manuscript drafts on time. (*wince* Sorry, Aimee.)

Haitian Vodou is an offspring of Vodun, the ancient West African religion that originated in several countries, including present-day Benin and Togo. Enslaved Africans may have lost their motherland, but they refused to be spiritually orphaned. Haitian Vodou, among other Diasporic offshoots of Vodun, was borne from that survival instinct, and it was practiced for protection and guidance while keeping practitioners connected to the ways of their ancestors.

Brooklyn's West Indian Day Parade felt like the perfect backdrop for this story. Not only because I have vivid memories of dancing down Eastern Parkway on Labor Days past, but because Carnival, like Haitian Vodou, involves a fusion of inherited and adopted traditions reshaped and repurposed by life under colonialsm. I also took a few liberties of reshaping Vodou in the hands of Tati Mimose and Mama Margo, and in using "Erzu" as a nickname for the lwa (spirit) Erzulie/Ezili.

Similar to the age-old religious notion that Vodou is not of God, there is a cultural notion that Haitians must strenuously disassociate from the stereotype that we're all practitioners of Vodou. During the writing of this book, I was agonizingly aware of my religious and cultural trespasses, and a small part of me did indeed monitor the sky for approaching lightning strikes.

I live whole states away from family, and I usually write hundreds of miles from them. Out of sight, out of mind, right? Funnily enough, I worked on revisions of this novel during my extended stay with family in Atlanta, New Jersey, and Brooklyn. And as I drafted this author's note, relatives were visiting me in Ohio. If lightning was going to strike me during the making of this book, my family were close by enough to get zapped, too.

Through this book, I pose the same questions that I challenged my beloved mom with as a teen during our infamous debates about my decision to wear my hair natural. *Why is it viewed negatively? Why must we shun it?* Similarly, I hope that readers reflect on these questions and are inspired to look into the answers.

When I stopped regularly straightening my hair as a teen, I understood why my family was against this. They only wanted my life to flow with as much ease as possible. They knew that I had to grow up and find employment, plus support myself financially. And sadly, wearing straight strands was viewed as putting my best face forward not only as a Black woman but as a public representative of my family and of Black people. The same could've been said about me writing about Vodou. My loved ones want my afterlife to be as dope as possible, and they knew that when I had to pass on one day and meet my Maker, shunning Vodou would help me ease past those pearly gates and be accepted into heaven.

But ironically, I never went on to work in corporate America, and my Maker made me with coily hair and an interrogating heart. Furthermore, today my work requires me to share from the heart.

Remind me never to touch this topic again, I emailed my editor as I teetered on the edge of another missed deadline. *Unless it's for a TV show. #ineverlearn*

But the absolute truth is, no matter what, I will continue to touch, poke, wrestle with, and embrace this topic. Like coily hair, it's my nature. And there's a strong tug in me to engage with matters of spirituality and ritual—if not in practice, at least in my storytelling and in the pages of my books.

Much love and many thanks to my always supportive family, friends, colleagues, and readers for their encouragement throughout my research process. And a special mèsi to Dr. Cécile Accilien for her keen, scholarly eye and her solid-gold notes. Every consultation and conversation I've had with the people I'm privileged to know has elevated this wild ride of an adventure story and amplified its thumping heartbeat. Thank you.

ABOUT THE AUTHOR

Debbie Rigaud is the author of the acclaimed YA novels *Simone Breaks All the Rules* and *Truly Madly Royally,* and the coauthor of Alyssa Milano's Hope series, which debuted on the *New York Times* bestseller list. Debbie grew up in East Orange, New Jersey, and started her career writing for entertainment and teen magazines. She now lives with her husband and children in Columbus, Ohio. Find out more at debbierigaud.com.

Check out more irresistible reads from Debbie Rigaud!

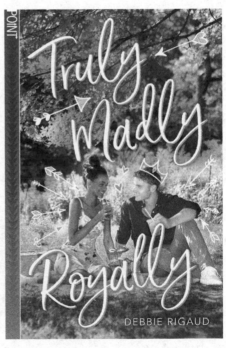